KEEP FLYING HIGH!

Bobby Nash '09

CORNERSTONE BOOK PUBLISHERS

NEW EDITION •UPDATED & RE-EDITED
AN AIRSHIP 27 PRODUCTION

Airship 27 Presents
"LANCE STAR: Sky Ranger" Volume 1
Edited by Ron Fortier
Lance Star is copyright © 2008 by Bobby Nash

"Introduction" copyright © 2008 by Norman Hamilton
"Attack of the Bird Man" copyright © 2008 by Frank Dirscherl
"Where the Sea Meets The Sky" copyright © 2008 by Bobby Nash
"Shadows over Kunlun" copyright © 2008 by Win Scott Eckert
"Talons of the Red Condors" copyright © 2008 by Bill Spangler
"Pulp Aviation Heroes & the Rise of the Model Aviation Press" copyright © 2008 by
 Larry Marshall
"Afterword" copyright © 2008 by Ron Fortier
"Runner" copyright © 2008 by Bobby Nash

Cover and interior illustrations copyright © 2008 by Rich Woodall
Lance Star logo design by Matt Talbot
Production and design by Rob Davis

All rights reserved under International and Pan-American Copyright
Conventions. No part of this book may be reproduced in any manner without
permission in writing from the copyright holder, except by a reviewer, who
may quote brief passages in a review.

Published by Cornerstone Book Publishers
New Orleans, Louisiana
www.cornerstonepublishers.com

ISBN: 1-934935-01-8
       978-1-934035-01-9

First Cornerstone Book Publishers Edition

Printed in the United States of America

10 9 8 7 6 5 4 3 2 1

Contents

CORNERSTONE BOOK PUBLISHERS

Introducing
LANCE STAR : SKY RANGER
by Norman Hamilton

In the summer of 1936 a new flying hero magazine was created called *Lance Star: Sky Ranger.* It was produced by the small time Canadian publisher, Dutton Press out of Ontario. Manager Editor, Saul Kingman, wanted a monthly to compete with the flying titles popping up all over the U.S. He wanted a title that would join the ranks of such heroes as *G-8, Dusty Ayers & Bill Barnes.*

Kingman hired pulp writer Owen Brown to create the new series. He would write 36 of the 48 *Lance Star* adventures that were presented as being penned by Chance Hunter.

Owen was the oldest son of Colonel Charles "Chuck" Brown who had flown with the French Squadrons in World War I and was the youngest pilot to have achieved ace status.

Owen, and his two brothers were all accomplished fliers by the time they left high school.

Owen Brown was a capable writer, having worked in New York City for many years contributing to many pulps of various genres. When he received the offer from Kingman, it didn't take him long to pack his bags and head north.

Initially there was some discussion about making *Lance Star* a Canadian, but the publisher, Roland Duquette, nixed that idea immediately. He wanted the new series to attract American readers. To have the same theme of patriotism the other series catered to. The rest was left to Brown's imagination. He set about swiping every conceivable concept he could find.

Lance Star is a blond-haired, handsome fellow who owns and operates an airfield outside of New York City. It was clearly modeled after the real Bennet Field in Long Island. He, like Doc Savage, was a genius inventor and his adventures always spotlighted some kind of new, fantastic aircraft. Although he had a home base, Lance's adventure took him all over the globe. The more exotic the locations, the wilder the tales.

He, too, was surrounded by a group of flying companions. Several of these, Buck Tellonger, Jack Falcone, and Walt Anderson were all older veterans who had flown in World War I. Red Davis was Lance's boyhood chum. Not only had they grown up together, but both had gone to flight school together. Then there was sophisticated Jim Nolan, a British flyer who signed up with Star because he craved adventure. The youngest member of Star's outfit was Skip Terrel. Lance was romantically involved with Skip's older sister, Betty.

Like all classic heroes, Star also had several colorful arch rivals. The deadliest of these was the Austrian, Baron Otto Von Blood. More on him in a bit. But the one villain who made the most appearances in the series was fellow American ace turned mercenary, Morgan Jones. Jones was a spoiled rich kid from California who grew up looking for cheap thrills anywhere he could find them. Using his family's wealth, he hired a squadron of rogue pilots whose only loyalty was to him. Star first encountered Morgan Jones in China, where he was working for an opium warlord, helping him to transport his deadly cargo to major eastern ports. Titled *"The Angel of Death"* and dated April 1937, it proved to be one of the most popular episodes in the magazine's history. At the end of the tale, Jones managed to escape Star and the Sky Rangers, vowing to return some day.

Now known by that very title, at reader demand, the character would come back to plague the Sky Rangers in a total of eight adventures.

During 1937 and 1938, the series did extremely well, holding its own in sales figures against its American competitors. The flying craze inspired by real-life heroes like Charles Lindbergh and Wiley Post kept the public reading by the thousands. There were even Lance Star Flying Clubs started all over America and Canada. But like all popular fads, it too began to wane and sales started to slack off.

Nothing unusual for big publishers, but for a little outfit like Dutton, it was a very serious matter. In a desperate attempt to shake things up, Kingman and Brown decided to kill off one of Star's crew. They chose Skip. The hue and cry of the readers was overwhelming.

The Dutton offices were flooded for months after *"Red Skies Over The Rhine,"* dated Feb. 1939, appeared on the stands. In the story, Lance and Skip travel to Germany at the government's request. There they discover the Blood Baron has assembled a secret air corps with the latest innovations at his disposal. His dream is to reclaim the lost glories of the Fatherland. The story foreshadowed the birth of the Luftwaffe and eventual rise of the Third Reich. Brown, like all his peers, was well aware of the world situation and the rumblings from overseas. In the climax, the Baron is about to shoot Lance in the back when Skip steps between them and takes the bullet meant for his friend. Lance spins around and shoots the Baron. Skip dies in his arms. It was heavy drama.

Although vehemently denouncing the death of one of their favorite characters, the readers came back and sales remained steady until the start of World War II. Saul Kingman passed away in 1943 of a heart attack. His replacement was Mort Brubaker, who would stay with the title until it folded in 1944. He and Brown never got along. Tired of constant rewrites Brubaker would impose on him, Owen left the series. He was replaced by several well known pulp writers; among them Paul Chadwick and Edward Olsen.

Brown and his brothers, John and Dale, all went to England and joined the RAF, were they distinguished themselves fighting against the Blitzkreig. Captain John Brown was shot down over France in November of 1944.

After the war, a decorated Owen Brown returned to his hometown of Jericho, New York where he married Barbara Sinclair. Finding most of the pulps had died out while he was overseas, Brown decided to try his hand at journalism and was hired by the *Jericho Tribune*. He never gave up his love of flying and he and brother Dale began the Long Island Bombers, a club for flying enthusiasts.

In 1949, Owen, Barbara and their first child, Grace, moved to Quincy, Massachusetts, where Brown took over as Managing Editor of the *Quincy Monitor,* a position he would hold for the twenty years

Owen Brown, c. 1937

until his retirement in 1979. He and Barbara had a total of three children; Grace, Claire and Daniel. During his later years, Owen was contacted by many pulp fans and did many interviews for various fanzines. Barbara says he toyed with the idea of writing an autobiography, but in the end thought it would be a waste of time, that no one was interested in the life of an ex-pulp writer-aviator.

Owen Brown died November 5th, 1986 at the age of 73.

As for Dutton Press, they continued to exist publishing women's titles and true crime periodicals. In 1965 the company closed its doors for the last time, unable to compete with the flashier US magazines. Henri Duquette, the only son of the company's founder, continued to manage the properties. After the sale of the factory and presses, he sold all magazine rights to NeverEnding Concepts, a New Hampshire based Multi-Media group. The rights to *Lance Star-Sky Ranger* and a dozen other popular pulp characters were renewed at that time. This volume was first published with their kind permission.

In 2007, the rights to *Lance Star-Sky Ranger* were transferred to writer Bobby Nash of Atlanta, GA. This new edition is published with his gracious support.

✦ Lance Star ✦

Attack of the Bird Man

by
Frank Dirscherl

Chapter 1

Lance Star groaned, lifted his head and peered through bleary eyes. He thought he'd heard a noise, heard something—or someone—interrupting him from his deserved gloom. He saw nothing, and plopped back down on his bunk. It had been months since the youngest member of his flying squadron, Skip Terrel, had perished, and Lance had spent his whole time since then in mourning. In reality, he'd done nothing at all, and the rest of his team had long expressed their grave concerns for him.

"Damn it, Lance, get up!" ordered Buck Tellonger who, along with the rest of the team—Red Davis, James Nolan and Kevin McDouglas—stood inside the door of the living room of Lance's bungalow on Star Field, Long Island.

"Get the hell out of here," Lance said in a raised voice, without moving from his bunk.

"Look at him," Buck snorted, "he can't even deign to look at us."

At this, Lance sat up, and stared at the sight of his squadron angrily staring at him. "What are you all doing here? I told you I didn't want to be disturbed."

"For five months?" asked Buck, incredulous. "You've neglected your duties, you've neglected your friends."

Lance shot upright, furious. He rubbed the full beard he had allowed to grow during his inertia. "How dare you judge me! We lost one of our own...Skip..." His voice drifted off into sorrow.

"Look," Buck started, clearly the designated leader of the group, "we all loved the lad. We all miss him. But, you can't go on like this. You're letting yourself, and everything around you, fall apart. Skip wouldn't have wanted you to kill yourself with grief."

Lance stood there, his mind reeling. A moment more of confusion, then he came to himself, realized blankly that it was almost as though he had been staring through his teammates rather than at them. Finally, he responded. "Maybe you're right," he said weakly. He rubbed his eyes and ran his fingers through his unkempt hair. "I just don't know anymore."

Kevin, the old Scotsman who was Lance's head technician, moved alongside Lance and helped him sit back down on his bunk. "It's okay, Lance, it's okay. We're here for you, you can turn to us."

Lance turned to face his old friend. "Thank you," he said, and smiled wanly. Jim Nolan sat down on Lance's other side, and offered a reassuring hand.

"We've managed—just—to keep everything afloat in your absence... but, you need to pull yourself together, for our sake as well as yours," said Buck.

Buck started to move slowly toward Lance, when Tony Lamport, the chief radio operator and superintendent of communications on Star Field, burst in, frantic, panting uncontrollably.

"Tony, what the hell?!" Buck said angrily.

"The radio...it's all over the radio," was all Tony could get out, indicating the wireless on the nearby sideboard.

Carrot-topped Red Davis was nearest the wireless, and he quickly switched it on. The frenzied tones of the newscaster blurted out the following:"The seaside town of Sarrayota in Northern California has experienced a remarkable and shocking series of events. Birds of every size and variety have attacked the town and its people. Details are still sketchy, but we're getting reports of at least some people being injured in the attack, and authorities are mystified to explain the cause. And now to local news—"

Red Davis switched the wireless off. Everyone was stunned by the news, and looked to Lance, if not for an explanation, then for some sign or direction. Lance sat there, stone-faced. After months of lethargy, months of feeling nothing but pain and sorrow and guilt, now Lance felt another strong emotion welling inside him. He'd often wondered if he would ever feel anything but grief again. He had his answer.

"Well," Kevin said, finally breaking the silence of the moment, "that was rather shocking."

Lance stood abruptly, catching everyone off guard. "Get the Skybolt ready. I'm heading for California." And he strode from the room into the adjoining suite without saying another word.

* * * * *

The squadron members, now alone in the bungalow, looked to each other with perplexed glances. Buck shrugged his shoulders, as if to say how should I know what's going on?

"At least he's up and moving," Buck said. "Let's just go with it, this may be the best thing for him."

The squadron dispersed, eager to do as Lance bade, ready to accept Buck's word on the subject. Buck remained behind, wanting to talk further with Lance. An instant later, and Lance appeared from the suite, outfitted in his usual flying garb. Apart from the thick beard he still wore, he looked his usual self—strong, tall, determined, albeit a little red-eyed. Buck couldn't help but smile.

"I can't tell you how good it is to see you like this again, Lance," he said. "There was a time when I never thought I'd see you in action again."

Lance stopped short, and smiled briefly at his Chief of Staff. "I want you with me, Buck."

Buck took Lance's arm, sat him down on the bunk. "Are you sure you want to rush off like this? Are you sure you're not replacing one extreme situation for another?"

Lance looked squarely into Buck's eyes. "Would that be so bad? I would have thought you'd be happy to have something take my mind off...off..." He couldn't go any further.

"I am, I am. I just...I just want you to be ready for this. You've barely moved from this bungalow in months. You're under done,"

Buck said.

Lance stood, determination etched into his handsome features. He headed for the front door. "No time. You heard the report. We need to get over there as quickly as possible to start an investigation."

"But we don't know that there's a need for an investigation. This could be a one-off, this could be nothing at all. Perhaps the authorities already have the situation well in hand," Buck said, following Lance out into the sunshine of a beautiful summer day.

"No, my gut tells me otherwise," said Lance, walking toward the main hangar on Star Field. "I can't explain it, but all I know is that I need to get over to Sarrayota and check this out personally."

And that was that as far as Buck was concerned.

* * * * *

Entering the hangar, the Skybolt rolled toward them, being pulled along by a truck driven by Red and Kevin.

"She's all ready, Lance," Kevin called out, beaming proudly. As Lance's head technician and chief mechanic, it was his responsibility to ensure all of Lance's planes and equipment were well maintained. The silver Skybolt shone with a brilliance all its own.

"Buck's coming with me," Lance stated, as Buck retreated to the rear of the hangar to get ready for the trip.

"Lance, you sure you don't want to try the new Pacer? She's complete and fully tested," Kevin said of the futuristic new plane Lance had designed and built. "She's a real beauty and made for speed."

"No, I need the Skybolt's new fuel capabilities for such a long trip. Besides, I feel more comfortable with her."

Kevin nodded, paused briefly before speaking up. "Lance, do you think this is the right thing to do right now?" Kevin asked.

Lance raised his hands in a stop signal. "Buck and I have gone through this. We're going."

The flying ace walked past the truck, toward his Skybolt. As the sun now caught the side of the craft, reflecting sharply off the shiny new paintwork, Lance briefly inspected the plane's onboard weaponry, which was considerable.

"Have the new fuel tanks been installed?" he asked Kevin.

"Installed, though not fully tested yet. It took us so long to connect the three new auxiliary tanks to the main tank...we just haven't been able to properly test her in the air yet."

"Today's a good day for it," Lance said, as he stepped up to and plopped into the pilot's seat.He'd invented a new fuel system not long before Skip's death, one that enabled the Skybolt to remain in the air for much longer periods than it ordinarily would be able to without need for refueling. Located near the rear of the plane, three new fuel tanks, which would pump fuel into the main tank automatically as that tank began to run dry. It was a unique and totally beneficial invention of Lance's that, amongst most other things in his life, he'd forced from his mind during his months of grief. The flying ace had confidence in his own abilities and that of Kevin. He had no doubt the new fuel system would work as designed and built.

"Well, everything looks just fine and dandy," Buck said, now outfitted in his flight-wear. He climbed into the other seat and got comfortable.

"Keep an eye on things here," Lance said to Red, who had remained close by. "I have this horrible feeling this bird attack is only the beginning."

Chapter 2

The Skybolt cut through the air like a mechanized knife through butter, its central propeller making quick work of the incredible distance already traveled. Over a picturesque mix of farmland, forests, mountains and towns, Lance and Buck whizzed by, intent on discovering what they could in the village of Sarrayota.

As they sped westward, now soaring 25,000 feet above the plains of Iowa, Lance heard Buck's voice barking over the intercom system.

"Lance, can you hear me?"

"Yes, coming through loud and clear."

"Lance...what do you think we'll find in Sarrayota?" Buck queried.

"I honestly don't know," Lance replied. "I can only hope there'll be some clues to point us in the right direction. Birds have never been known to attack man as wantonly as reported. Something is—" He stopped short.

"What? What's wrong?" Buck said.

"It's just occurred to me...but, we haven't seen one bird since we left Star Field. Not one."

"You're right," Buck started. "I hadn't noticed, but you're right. What can that mean?"

"I don't know, Buck. But I don't like it."

Lance geared his controls forward, pushing the Skybolt as hard as he could. He wanted to get there as quickly as possible. The situation there was gnawing at him. Something was telling him that the attack in Sarrayota was merely a precursor, that something much more serious was looming on the horizon. And it was that thought that chilled him to the bone.

* * * * *

Sarrayota emerged in the distance, as the warm summer sun began its slow but steady descent into sunset. The brilliant, orange display bathed the sleepy seaside town in a hue that was truly breathtaking. It was hard to believe that a town like this was the scene of such horror a mere twenty-four hours earlier.

"Can you see any landing area?" Buck spat out over the plane's intercom system.

"There," Lance responded, pointing to a small airfield to his right. He banked the plane in that direction, and quickly guided the Skybolt down to a steady and assured landing.

"How happy do you think the authorities will be to see us?" Buck asked, as Lance lifted the Skybolt's canopy. "You know local sheriffs often don't like outside help treading on their toes."

"I'm sure we'll get by just fine," Lance said, hopping onto the patchy grass and soil of the airfield, little more than a flattened area of dusty farmland.

They trudged over to the minuscule hangar at the far end of the runway, and were met by a grizzled old man, obviously the man in charge there. "You wanna park yer airplane here? It'll cost you."

"No problem. Handle this will you," he indicated to Buck.

Lance walked over to the end of the property, which overlooked the town itself, which in turn was situated down the rise some, hugging the ocean at the center of the bay there. The sight of the village again impressed upon Lance the image of a sleepy, peaceful habitat. What he would find there he knew not, but he intended to not tarry any longer.

"What is it, Lance?" Buck asked, having now joined the flying ace's side.

"Let's get down there," he replied.

The walk down the hill was a relatively easy one. They decided to avoid the snaking dirt road and cut across a series of emerald pastures, before reaching the base of the ridge and the edge of town. The sun had now set, and as they walked down what appeared to be Sarrayota's main thoroughfare—if one could call it that—the meager building's began casting strange, ominous shadows down the town's narrow streets.

"We need to find the sheriff's office," Lance directed. "I'd like to know more before we get into it in full tomorrow morning."

After asking directions from a local, they soon arrived at the sheriff's office and marched up the few steps leading inside the small, timbered building.

"Sorry, we're about to close," a small, uniformed man with rounded glasses said without looking up from his desk. "Unless it's an emergency, come back tomorrow."

"I'm afraid this can't wait," Lance said, his strong, deep voice rousing the sheriff from his work.

"Oh my gosh," the sheriff said in amazement. "Are you him? Are you really him?"

Buck took a forward step and smiled. Lance knew his friend was always proud of the recognition he received wherever he went.

"Yes, it's us...Lance Star and his incredible assistant, Buck Tellonger," Buck said, beaming.

The sheriff rounded his desk, ignoring Buck. A grin of gigantic proportions never left his narrow face. "I didn't recognize you at first with that beard, but I'd know you anywhere. I've been your biggest fan for years," the sheriff blurted. "How you stopped that Angel of Death, I'll never know. Wait until I tell my son about who came into my office tonight."

Lance smiled, blushed slightly. Fame was never something he'd yearned for, but it came with the territory, and he accepted that. Nevertheless, it was something he had never become completely comfortable with.

"Thank you, Sheriff..."

"Majors," the sheriff replied.

"Sheriff Majors, we're here to look into yesterday's bird attack," Lance revealed, his demeanor becoming much more serious.

"Oh..." the sheriff said, his attitude suddenly changing. The little man shifted uncomfortably in the gaze of the two flying aces. "Why would that interest you?"

"I would think it would interest anyone who puts the public interest ahead of their own," Buck said pointedly.

"Let's just say," Lance added, "that I could do with the distraction right now. And I sense a great danger here."

The sheriff scratched his head, his fingers moving rhythmically through his thin, graying hair, his face clouding over with concern. "Look, don't get me wrong...I'm appreciative of any help and advice you can provide, it's just that...everyone I've talked to about this from the outside world thinks I'm crazy."

"Is that why I saw no authorities in the town? No signs of any outside assistance?" Lance probed.

"But, we heard the reports on the radio, there was no mention of it being a joke or a hoax," Buck said.

"Oh, the reports of the bird attack are being taken at face value, and that much of the story has been accepted as the God's truth. Enough people saw what happened to assure everyone of that fact," Sheriff Majors explained. "And we lost two of our own..." The sheriff appeared to drift into sadness before pulling himself together. "But there was more to yesterday's attack. Much more."

"I don't understand," Lance said, confused.

The sheriff swallowed hard before continuing. "We weren't just attacked by birds yesterday...I also saw a bird as big as a man, in the sky, controlling the other birds. A Bird Man."

Chapter 3

A Bird Man. Those words sent chills down Lance's spine. How could that be possible? A bird as big as a man? Impossible. And yet...

"What are you saying? A bird the size of a man? Or—" Lance inquired.

"I'm saying it was some kind of a creature. Gold help me, but I saw it with my own eyes. So did a few others in town. I couldn't honestly say whether it were a man or animal..." the sheriff said, tapering off.

Buck looked to Lance, pulled a face that the sheriff evidently caught.

"I know, I know. You think I'm as crazy as the Feds do. That's why they refused to send anyone out here. They barely believed the reports of the bird attack, until they heard from others in the town who verified my story. I'm actually surprised they didn't send the guys in white coats after me."

"Let's sit down," Lance offered, pointing to the series of chairs in the small waiting room section of the office. "Now, tell me what happened. I need to know everything."

* * * * *

"...a flock of seagulls began wantonly attacking anyone or anything that moved."

Early the next morning, before much of the town had come to life for the day, Lance, Buck and Sheriff Majors were out inspecting the sights of the various bird attacks that had taken place only two days earlier. The sheriff had detailed what had happened the night before, leaving both Lance and Buck incredulous, but determined to get to the bottom of the mystery. Lance was no avian expert, but he knew enough of the various species to know that they did not—would not—attack human beings unprovoked, and certainly not en masse as the sheriff had described.

Apparently, as the sheriff had detailed, around noon two days ago, while Sarrayota's citizens were innocently going about their daily business, a flock of seagulls began wantonly attacking anyone or anything that moved. Terrified shoppers fled the carnage, streaming into shops, cafés and restaurants. Housewives bunkered down in their homes, school children were sequestered in their classrooms. Windows were smashed, and a few minor car crashes were reported, but no one had been originally thought to have been seriously hurt. Then, almost as soon as the attack had started, the gulls retreated, and life returned to normal. It was only then, as the clean-up and investigation started, that the bodies of an elderly couple, pecked to death on their front porches, were discovered.

Subsequently, a mere few hours later, a flotilla of herons dive-bombed some schoolchildren on their way home from school. Miraculously none of the children were badly injured, bar some minor cuts and grazes. The herons then turned their assault on the village itself, terrifying the townsfolk once again, with the end result being as before—after some minutes, the birds retreated, and all was again as normal. Frantic calls to the sheriff had brought him out, but he had been unable to do anything except watch the bizarre goings-on. While hunkered in his car during the latter attack, he thought he caught sight of something incredibly large through his windshield. Risking injury, he stepped out to get a better view. What he saw chilled him to the bone—a bird the size and just about shape of a man, hovering in the sky high above. With a shrill cry that sent shivers down his spine, the Bird Man called, and the herons retreated instantly.

Fully apprised of the situation, the three of them were walking the streets, examining the specific areas where the birds caused the most damage—to property and to themselves—smashing up against walls, windows and the like.

"We've cleaned up all the birds already...oh, there's one we missed," the sheriff said, spying the carcass of a gull lying nearby.

Lance knelt down, looked at the bird intently, but didn't touch it. He could see nothing obviously wrong with the poor creature's body, apart from its self-sustained wounds, and stood soon thereafter.

"What do you think?" Sheriff Majors asked.

"I don't see anything out of the ordinary with this bird, though I'm no expert. I suggest doing some lab work on its blood, see if that shows up anything of significance."

They then proceeded to view the damage caused by the birds throughout the town. It was extensive. Broken or cracked windows were the most common, but there were still some wrecked cars strewn about, caused no doubt by the drivers losing control of their vehicles during the carnage. Some chimneys were also partially crumbled atop the village's little houses. They even interviewed several of the villagers, who vividly recounted the horrifying events of a mere forty-eights hours previous. And, they found three people who confirmed the sight of the Bird Man, repeating the story of the sheriff almost verbatim.

By the afternoon, the three were seated inside the sheriff's office, Lance seriously mulling over all he had learned and seen during the day.

"Well," Lance started, "we've gone over the eyewitness testimony, and we've seen the evidence of the attacks firsthand."

"And?" the sheriff asked, hopeful.

"I cannot explain this. I see no reason why the birds would behave this way. And, if they were under the control of this...Bird Man, then how was this achieved? I know of no way to control birds of differing species in such large numbers and to such an exacting degree as has been evidenced here."

The sheriff looked downcast. No doubt he'd hoped for results of some kind, and Lance felt for him. He asserted there and then to redouble his efforts in solving the town's predicament.

Lance sighed. "I'm sorry we don't have any answers—yet. But..."

"It's okay," the sheriff said. "Maybe I am going mad after all... maybe this whole town is."

"Well, it's getting late, and I'm starving," Buck said, sounding more upbeat. "Any place we can go and grab some dinner?"

"Sure, try Ralph's Diner by the wharf. Best fish & chips in California," Sheriff Majors said, smiling somewhat.

Lance and Buck exited the sheriff's office and made their way through Sarrayota's narrow, picturesque streets toward the wharf, where Ralph's Diner was located. There were a few people about, but they appeared somewhat furtive, perhaps a little less than friendly. Lance made a mental note but said nothing to Buck. Such thoughts continued sifting through his mind as he and Buck arrived at the diner, which they then entered.

The diner was very rustic, simple but airy, and was about half full. As they walked through the restaurant toward a corner booth at the rear, Lance and Buck noticed the customers' attention trained on them, which they ignored and took their chosen seats. A pretty, young waitress soon approached them.

"Are you gentlemen ready to order?"

"Roast beef dinner and coffee for me," Lance said. "And the veal and a pot of tea for my friend here."

The waitress retreated, leaving Lance and Buck alone, with much of the customers' attention still focused on them.

"I'm not sure we're exactly wanted here," Buck whispered.

"You might be right," Lance replied, scanning the diner's patrons while doing so. "Though I can't imagine why."

Before another word could be spoken, one of the patrons stood and approached their table. He was an elderly man with grayish wisps of hair emerging from under a stained, peaked cap. His eyes penetrated piercingly from above small, horn-rimmed glasses.

"I hear yer here about them birds," the man said.

"That's right," Buck replied. "Do you have any information for us?"

"Yeah," the man started. "I have some information for ya...leave us alone."

"Sir, we're here to help," Lance said.

"We don't need yer help, we don't need anything. This was nothing, one of them freaks of nature," the man said forcefully.

"We've heard reports of a—"

"Bird Man, right?" the man snapped. "Ya don't believe that guff do ya?"

"I don't know," Lance said. "But I know it's worth investigating."

"There's nothing to investigate. Just leave us alone. We can take care of ourselves." He paused, before finishing, "I advise you to leave quickly."

With that, the man spun on his heels and marched from the diner. Lance watched him do so, noting something curious about the man, but not able to pinpoint what it was that bothered him at that moment. At that, the customers' attentions reverted back to their own food and company.

"What's going on here, Lance?" Buck said, scratching his head.

"Honestly...I have no idea. But I intend finding out."

After a few minutes of quiet contemplation, the young waitress delivered their meals. While Lance and Buck began tucking in to their delicious tasting food, a young mother pushing her child's pram tore into the diner, sheer panic etched onto her attractive features.

"My God! It's happening again," she screamed.

Lance shot to his feet and raced over to the woman. "The birds?"

She was pale with fright and could say nothing more. She pointed outside, and Lance's gaze followed her directions, out through the diner's large, double-glass door. What he saw shocked even him—birds, at least dozens of them, of varying varieties, swooping down at people, cars...and now toward the diner itself.

Chapter 4

A flock of crows crashed violently into the diner's glass door, cracking it. The noise of the carnage outside sent the diner's patrons scuttling, some down under their tables, others retreating to the rear of the building, their terror palpable. Buck soon joined Lance at the diner's entrance.

"The sheriff didn't exaggerate," said Buck, straining to see as much of the bird attack as possible. "What are we going to do?"

"Look," Lance cried out, pointing.

There, across the street, was a largish, middle-aged man fighting to get back into his car, but the crows were diving at him, pecking him ferociously as he began to slump to the ground, his right arm still clutching the car's door handle.

There wasn't a moment to lose. Lance rushed out into the street, shielding himself from the crows' attack as best he could. Sprinting, he quickly reached the plump man, who was clearly weakened from the combined effects of gaping wounds to the face and hands, and the terror of the moment. Lance helped the poor man inside his car. The flying ace crouched there, beating the birds away with as much strength as he could muster. From his current position, it was as though the sky was blotted out, all he could see were the birds now bearing down upon him. The creatures squawked and cawed their presence, their cries ringing in Lance's ears.

Lance fought back bravely, but despite the effort, he too was soon marked from the birds' sharp claws and beaks. He wondered if he shouldn't get up into the car himself, into some measure of safety, but then the birds reacted, rose a short distance into the air, circled and returned to the heavens from whence they came.

Lance watched with fascination and a feeling of horror soon overcame him. For there, high in the sky, was the Bird Man itself. Lance couldn't help rubbing his eyes, but the sight of the creature, hovering there menacingly, failed to disappear as his vision cleared. Though a long way up, Lance's vision was particularly acute, and he could clearly make the creature, whatever it was, out.

"Oh my God," Buck uttered, now by Lance's side.

"Quickly, we can't let it escape," Lance said, who was up like a shot. "We need to be airborne as quickly as possible."

He ran down the street, with Buck at his heels. They were racing for the Skybolt, parked as it was on the hillside airstrip just outside town. As they sprinted through Sarrayota, Lance could clearly hear Buck panting behind him, never losing touch with his powerful strides.

Lance craned his head skyward, caught sight of the Bird man still hovering, as though it were watching for its entire flock to escape safely from Sarrayota. Good, Lance thought. That gives us time to reach the Skybolt and pursue it.

They reached the hill, and desperately scrambled up it, not wishing to waste any more time than was absolutely necessary. Lance's powerful legs carried his muscular frame upward, reaching the crest in mere minutes. But were we fast enough? Lance again scanned the sky, spotting the Bird Man in, what he estimated, to be the same position as before. Good.

Lance and Buck sped past the grizzled attendant, jumping up into the Skybolt with the ease of those completely familiar with such a craft. Lance instantly fired the engine to life, and rumbled the machine down the bumpy airstrip runway. As quickly as possible, they were airborne, and speeding in the direction Lance last saw the Bird Man.

They weren't in the air a minute or two before they spotted the Bird Man up ahead.

"There," Lance's voice barked through the Skybolt's intercom system.

Amazingly, the flock of crows were nowhere to be seen, but the Bird Man itself remained, eerily hovering in place. As the Skybolt sped toward it, its immense size and shape became clearer, and Lance could hear Buck's gasps of amazement at the sight of the creature. It was large, at least 7 feet tall by Lance's estimation, shaped more-or-less like a man, though with the face of a bird; a hideous, sharp beak and the piercing eyes of a hawk, as well as being covered head to tow in brown-hued plumage, which gave the creature its birdlike appearance, animalistic in a most aggressive fashion. It looked like nothing else on Earth.

"It's just hanging there, as though it were waiting for us," Buck said.

The creature eyed the approaching Skybolt with contemptuous, piercing eyes, but remained still, it's only movement the slight beating of its wings. Lance was intrigued...how could it stay aloft, keeping such a weight airborne, with such slight movement of its wings? An answer, however, was not forthcoming. Now practically upon the creature, it turned, and shot away from the flying aces with incredible speed.

"Holy..." Buck said under his breath. "I've never seen such speed on a..."

"We can't let it get away," Lance ordered, and he pushed the Skybolt onward as hard as he could.

The pursuit was fast and furious, and Lance thought for a few moments that they were gaining on the Bird Man. But it was a brief and forlorn hope. In minutes, the creature had vanished from sight, merging into the darkening horizon from whence it apparently came.

Lance pulled back on the controls, frustrated at having lost the creature so easily. He slammed his fist on the console.

"Dammit!" he said.

"Easy, Lance, easy," Buck responded.

"It was playing with us...it knew we couldn't match it for speed, and played us for fools."

"It's just hanging there, as though it were waiting for us,"

There was a moment of silence, as Lance contemplated their next course of action. Lance clutched the controls, prepared to turn the Skybolt back toward Sarrayota, when he heard Buck gasp in horror.

"Oh my God!" Buck uttered.

Lance looked up, and saw the reason for Buck's reaction. The Bird Man was knifing through the air toward them, at unimaginable speed, on a collision course with them. Lance yanked at the controls, sending the Skybolt careening to the left, as the large mass of the Bird Man swooped up and over them. The sickening sound of metal grating on metal could be heard as the plane spiraled out of control. Lance seized the stick with all his strength, and managed to finally bring the craft back under control.

"Buck, any sign of the Bird Man?" Lance inquired.

Buck, obviously shaken by the incident, soon replied. "Nothing, I can't see it anywhere. It's gone."

Lance circled several times, hoping to catch sight of the creature once more, but it appeared to have truly escaped...for now.

* * * * *

Lance brought the Skybolt down at the small Sarrayota airstrip. The bristled, elderly attendant appeared from the small hangar, removed his cap and scratched his head at the sight of the plane. Lance wondered at his reaction.

Bringing the Skybolt to a halt, Lance and Buck slowly exited and were met by the attendant.

"What in heckfire happened up there?" he questioned.

"What?" Buck said, bewildered.

The attendant shot out a grubby-sleeved arm, pointed up toward the Skybolt. Lance and Buck turned and finally saw what he meant. Moving up and over the Skybolt's rear was a large, gnawing scar in the metal itself. Lance climbed up to get a better look.

"Claw marks," he declared after a few moments. "Obviously the noise we heard when the Bird Man attacked." He jumped back down, his large frame plopping into the dirt.

"What kind of claw could do that to the body of the Skybolt?"

Buck queried. "Could that...that thing actually be real? I mean... could there actually be a Bird Man?"

The old attendant scratched his head again. "You're plum loco." He waved them off and retreated to the hangar.

Lance took his gloves off, and began wandering back toward town, with Buck by his side. He stroked his full beard in consternation.

"Something about this is not right," Lance said. "For a second there, I started to believe that creature was some freak of nature perhaps. But now...now I'm not so sure."

"What's changed your mind?" Buck probed, as the two began their descent into town.

"I don't know. Something I can't quite put my finger on yet. But I will. I will."

* * * * *

Lance had determined to inspect the various sites throughout Sarrayota where the birds had attacked again, and also wanted to check on the health of the man he had assisted. Thankfully, the man was fine, and eternally grateful to Lance for saving his life. Lance accepted the platitudes with his usual graciousness, and not a little humility.

Lance and Buck went on to inspect the damage done by the most recent bird attack. Perhaps not as extensive as the initial assault, or even the second, but what was damaged was often seriously so. Even in the dark, they could see the bodies of many crows lying scattered about the streets, their bloodied masses bearing testament to the war being waged on the town. Again, the dead birds offered no clues to Lance, and he soon joined Buck back at their guest house bungalow to mull over the evening's events.

"I can't believe what I've seen tonight," Buck said under his breath, seated on the small, plump couch. "I can't believe how much has happened in such a short space of time. I'm having trouble coming to terms with it all."

"I know how you feel," Lance replied, stroking his full beard. He was seated on the too-short camp bed opposite Buck. "But, I feel we've come some way with our investigation."

"We have?" Buck said, astounded. "Have I missed something?"

"The claw marks!" Lance said suddenly, standing bolt upright."That's it, that's what's been bugging me."

"Wha—?" was all Buck could muster, as Lance strode past him quickly, and exited through the bungalow's flimsy screen door.

Chapter 5

Lance and Buck were back at the airstrip, looking over the Skybolt in the pitch of night.

"What this all about, Lance?" Buck inquired. "Couldn't this wait until morning?"

Lance clambered up the plane, ignoring Buck's question. "Hold that light steady."

Buck complied, focusing the light of the lantern toward the claw marks located at the rear of the plane.

"What are you looking for?" Buck asked.

"There," Lance declared. "See this?" Lance pointed at a spot within the lengthy gash.

"Uhh...no."

"Move in closer," Lance said.

Buck did so, moving with the lantern as close to the plane, and the gash at its rear, as he could.

"See it now?" Lance asked.

"No. What am I looking at?"

"Can you see here?" Lance pointed at a specific spot. "See these small metallic fragments?" He brushed at them with his finger nail, and there was indeed some small, loose metallic fragments contained within the gash. "And they're not pieces of the Skybolt."

Recognition flashed on Buck's face. "I understand now. The Bird Man's claws were made of some kind of metal."

33

"A powerful alloy, I'd say, judging by the damage done, though I've never seen anything like it." Lance jumped back down to Earth. "We should have known from the sound of our collision in the air that something was not kosher...the significance of that and the gash here only dawned on me back at the bungalow."

"Okay, so we know we're dealing with a man here, not a creature," Buck outlined. "But where does that leave us now? It's a man...that only leaves us with more questions than before. How could a man take to the air without a plane? With what appears to be wings? Impossible! And yet, we both saw—"

"I have no answers for you, Buck," Lance interrupted, ruffling his hair. "But I can tell you this—I'm going to find out."

"I very much doubt that," a coarse, animalistic voice rang out from behind them. Lance and Buck whirled, and found themselves standing face-to-face with the Bird Man. How it had managed to arrive there without them hearing it, Lance could only wonder. Standing a way back from them, they could still make out its imposing shape and size in the weak light of the lantern.

"I advise you to leave quickly," the Bird Man said, its voice a powerful rasp. "Tonight, you escaped with your lives. Next time you may not be so fortunate."

Lance squinted through the low light, trying to gain a better view of the Bird Man. It was extremely tall, that much was clear, with an incredible wingspan, and powerful, authentic-appearing claws at the end of its long, man-like legs. Truly a vision of a beast from the most hellish of imaginations.

"And if we refuse?" Lance asked, trying to look and sound as courageous as possible.

The Bird Man emitted an eerie, almost otherworldly sound that can best be described as a mix between a growl and the attacking shriek of a bird of prey. Instantly, the Bird Man launched itself into the air, silently and with such speed as to be almost invisible in the darkness. Buck frantically waved his lantern about, vainly trying to spot it. Then, with a whoosh of air, Buck was yanked up off the ground, and he disappeared up into the stratosphere. The lantern crashed to the ground, leaving Lance Star completely alone.

"Buck!" he screamed, not quite panicking, but he doubted he'd ever been this close before. He retrieved the lantern and started waving it about, but found his efforts to be as fruitless as Buck's had been only moments before.

Then, Lance thought he heard something. His hearing was extremely acute, but this wasn't something tangible. What is that sound? As if in answer to that, the body of Buck came crashing down into the dirt with a thud. Tellonger groaned but remained still.

"Buck," Lance cried, rushing over to his friend's side. He looked him over as best he could by the light of the lantern—he didn't appear to be injured, but the fall had been a hefty one.

"That was but a warning," the Bird Man's voice grated from above. Lance strained to look up in the direction he estimated the voice was coming from, but saw nothing but the blackness of night and the light of the full moon attempting to penetrate the thick cloud cover. "Your assistant will tell you more." With a barely audible whoosh, Lance knew then that the Bird Man had vanished.

* * * * *

Back at their bungalow accommodation, Buck was lying down, recuperating from his ordeal. Lance sat next to him, waiting for him to feel ready to talk about what had happened. Buck was heavily bruised but otherwise appeared okay.

"I'm okay, Lance, you needn't fuss over me," Buck said, his ego apparently more battered than his body.

"What happened up there? The Bird Man said..."

"He's nuts, completely nuts," Buck began to outline. "He said his attacks on Sarrayota have merely been a prelude to a much larger attack on the west coast, as a way to illustrate the power he yields and the damage he's capable of causing. He intends wreaking as much havoc as he can, then will hold the country to ransom."

Lance sat bolt upright. "My God!"

"He flew higher than I've ever been before, Lance," Buck continued. "It's not possible for a man to go so high, but...I blacked out due to a lack of oxygen, I don't know what happened then, if anything. Next thing I knew, I was back on the ground nursing a sore behind."

Lance stood and began pacing the room. "Hmm...obviously he has some kind of breathing apparatus built into his...costume."Lance continued pacing. "There has to be a way to stop this carnage. If we allow it to escalate, I'm not sure we'd ever be able to stop it...and thousands of lives could be lost in the process."

Silence for a few moments, as the two of them contemplated the horror of Lance's words. Lance rubbed his chin and started pacing anew. "First things first.How is he able to take flight unaided? It can't be those wings alone, that's been tried in the past and proven to be an abject failure," Lance said, remembering the many efforts at flight man had attempted before and after the Wright Bros. fabled success. "It's a costume, of course."

"There have to be some mechanics involved," Buck said, sitting upright.

"Right," Lance replied. "But how? The Bird Man almost made no sound as it flew."

"I can't explain it," Buck finally said. "This has me totally flummoxed."

Lance continued with his pacing, though remained silent. From the corner of his eye, Lance saw Buck watching him for a time, before lying down and soon drifted off into a sound sleep. Lance smiled. No need to wake him after his ordeal tonight. He got his coat, and silently exited the bungalow.

* * * * *

Buck woke with a start. He'd had a nightmare that he was trapped in a giant bird's nest, with the Bird Man looming, hungry, its beak dripping with...

"Sheesh, what a nightmare," he said to himself softly, trying to shake the memory of it from his mind.

He rubbed his eyes, allowed his vision to clear, and found that he was alone in the tiny bungalow.

"Lance?" he said. There was no reply.

Buck stood, ruffled his hair, and looked around the bungalow for any sign of Lance's whereabouts. Lance's coat was missing, but other than that, there was nothing. Buck moved over to the door, peered out into the darkness. I mustn't have slept for very long, it's still night. There was no sign of Lance.

Buck scratched his head.Lance wouldn't have left without me unless he'd stumbled onto something, and...that's it, he's thought of something and couldn't wait to go test out his theory.

Buck grabbed his own coat and rushed out into the night. He shivered, for despite the coat, the temperature had dropped since their tangle with the Bird Man; a chill breeze had come in from the north and taken hold. He trudged through the town, keeping an eye out for any sign of Lance, but found none. Could he be back at the Skybolt? Might he have thought of some new clue? Buck decided to head there first, and think up his next move there based on what he might find.

* * * * *

The airstrip was deserted, the only sight or sound of life were the crickets chirping their nighttime presence. The northerly winds continued their barrage on Sarrayota, which caused Buck to shudder as he wrapped his coat's collar up around his neck. But there was no sign of Lance. Buck began to worry. While he knew and respected that Lance could take care of himself, he also knew the level of threat they were dealing with, and remembered the Bird Man's ominous warning. He shuddered again.

What do I do now? What would Lance do in such a situation?The questions bubbled around in Buck's brain as he searched for the answers. While he held his lantern aloft, searching for clues, a rustling sound caused him to jump. He whirled, and spotted the elderly man with the peaked cap from the diner.

"You startled me," Buck said, breathing a little easier, though disappointed it wasn't Lance. "What are you doing here?"

The elderly man stepped forward, an angry look on his face."I could say the same of ya," he said. "Didn't I warn ya to leave this town? Didn't I advise you to leave quickly?"

Buck took a step back, suspicion registering in his mind. What's up with this old coot? His speech.... "Mister, we'll leave when we've gotten to the bottom of this situation—not before."

The elderly man's features contorted in fury, and he rushed forward, growling in the process, causing Buck to drop his lantern in surprise. A harsh shove, and Buck was eating dirt. He'd had enough of that, he'd tasted it too often that night. He grunted in anger and frustration, getting to his feet promptly.

He stood there, trying to regain his composure and his thoughts. But the elderly man had vanished. What had just happened here? He tried to make sense of the insensible...then it hit him. The strange inconsistencies in the old man's speech, finding him at the airstrip in the middle of the night. Oh my God! The revelation hit him like a jackhammer. He rushed back down the hill toward town.

Chapter 6

Buck sprinted toward the sheriff's office. It was very early in the morning, still dark, but this was an emergency, and he only hoped he wouldn't be too late. With the now visible full moon high in the night sky, lighting his path, he caught sight of a large plume of smoke billowing from a nearby street.

"Oh no," he said to himself, and changed course, racing in the direction of the smoke. His gut was telling him his worst fears could well be realized...if only it weren't too late.

Two blocks from the sheriff's office, Buck reached the scene. A small timbered shack was fully ablaze. The shack's so small, nobody could still...no, he thought, there must still be hope.Thinking not of his own safety, Buck plunged headfirst through the shack's rickety front door, into the heart of the maelstrom. The shack was indeed fully ablaze, but inside, there were still small patches unaffected in which to move freely. Coughing, straining to see through the acrid inferno, Buck could just make out that the shack was larger, stretching backward, than was initially visible from the street. There was no sign of life within this small, front living area.

"Lance," he managed to cry out, his throat and lungs beginning to burn.

He pushed past some blazing debris—my God, the roof is starting to cave in—in his furious efforts to get to the rear of the shack.

He squeezed through a burning doorway, and entered a short,

dingy corridor. Thankfully, the flames had not yet reached this part of the shack. Obviously the fire had started at the front of the cabin.

"Lance, where are you?" Buck yelled again. He coughed, but tried hard to listen for any kind of a reply. With the fire raging uncontrollably behind him, that was not an easy task. But...what was that? He strained to hear as best he could. Muffled cries?They were coming from another room which lay up ahead.Buck hurried into the tiny bedroom. There, on a bare camp bed, lay Lance Star, tied up and gagged.

"Lance!" Buck said in exultation, happy and relieved to find his friend alive. Tellonger immediately produced a flick-knife, and freed Lance from his bonds in an instant. "What happened? I awoke to find you gone."

Lance stood, rubbed his wrists gingerly. "No time for that now, we have to get out of here."

The aviator took the lead, storming into the corridor heading for the shack's front—and apparently only—entrance. As he and Buck reached the doorway into the living area, the entire roof came crashing down in an explosion of flame and timber. Lance and Buck jumped back, raising their arms to shield themselves as best they could.Sparks shot toward them, singeing their arms, causing their clothes to slightly smolder.

"Back," Lance ordered, and they retreated into the still safe bedroom.

Buck took a peek back into the corridor, only to see the flames now moving quickly through the thoroughfare toward them.

"We're trapped," Buck said despairingly.

Lance pivoted, and then spotted the small, blackened and grimy window at the far end of the room. He motioned to it, and Buck knew instantly. Lance took a flying leap, knifing through the window with pinpoint precision. He landed hard amongst a raining of shattered glass fragments. Buck quickly followed, grunting as he landed beside Lance on the grass.

They gathered themselves, then moved a fair distance to safety. The sound of fire trucks approaching filled the air, as the two bent over, hacking good air back into their lungs.

"Thank God I found you in time," Buck finally said.

"Thank God you came when you did. I wouldn't have survived much longer," Lance said in reply, as the rear of the shack now came crashing down, the entire shanty having collapsed, burning with incredible intensity.

"Are you going to tell me what happened?" Buck quizzed, finally breathing a little easier.

"John Grissom...the elderly man who warned us at the diner. He's the Bird Man!"

* * * * *

Lance and Buck were now making their way back out to their parked Skybolt at the airstrip on the outskirts of town.

"I'd had this idea that the Bird Man was somehow using a strong magnetic field to power his wings, tapping into the Earth's natural magnetic structure, enabling him to somehow harness it for flight. That's why there was little or no sound when he flew," Lance outlined as they walked. "I thought to rig something up to counter that with the equipment in the Skybolt's electronics kit. When I arrived there, Grissom was waiting; he'd obviously followed me. As soon as I saw who it was, I knew instantly he was the Bird Man."

"It was his speech, right? He sounded like he was pretending to be less educated than he truly was. And he used the same words I advise you to leave quickly that the Bird Man used," Buck said, beaming.

"Right," Lance replied. "He's also not as old as he appears, that's a clever makeup trick. He got the jump on me at the airstrip—slugged me—and when I came to, I was a prisoner in his shack. It was there that he explained everything to me."

"Funny how these villains get more chatty when they think they have the upper hand," Buck said, as they made their way up the hill to the waiting Skybolt.

"Grissom was a former lieutenant of the Angel of Death," Lance continued, "which is where he gained his aviation knowledge. In truth, it was he who was largely responsible for the upkeep of that villain's equipment, and the inventor of the magnetic flying apparatus he now utilizes as the Bird Man."

"Your hunch was right then."

"Yes. Grissom was using Sarrayota as a test case, and disguised himself as a local inhabitant—one he'd murdered weeks ago—to gain firsthand knowledge of the effects the bird attacks were having on the townsfolk. That way, he was able to absorb their fear, their anxiety, and use that knowledge in future attacks along the coast."

"But how was he able to control all those birds?" Buck asked, the dawn sun just beginning to creep over the crest of the hill.

Before Lance could reply, suddenly appearing at the edge of the horizon in flocks from the east large enough to block out the rising sun, were birds, Lance estimated to number in their thousands.

"Oh no," Buck groaned. "How can we stop them now?"

Chapter 7

Lance wasted no more time, and ran over to the parked Skybolt. He climbed up, hurriedly opened the cockpit and dropped inside.

"Lance, what are you doing?" Buck asked.

Lance was reaching into the fuselage behind the rear cockpit, sifting through his emergency equipment. "Ah, here it is," he signaled, bringing forth the case that contained his electronics kit. Lance never traveled without it. "The only way to stop Grissom is to rig this anti-magnetism device I thought to try and build earlier. I only hope I can do so in time."

Lance worked feverishly as Buck watched on, despairing for Sarrayota as the birds came ever closer. The minutes dragged on like hours, deceptively so. Lance mopped the sweat from his brow, looked up to the sky at the looming terror, then looked over to Buck, who was finding it hard to keep still.

Lance kept at it, pulling apart certain electrical circuits, re-wiring others, and mixing it all into a weird concoction of equipment which looked as strange and unwieldy as a child's school science project.

"There," Lance finally proclaimed.

"But will that...thing work?" Buck asked, scrunching his nose at the sight of it.

"I don't know, but we don't have any time to argue about it. We need to get airborne. Now!"

He positioned the apparatus in the rear cockpit, as Buck leaped up onto the Skybolt's wing, and moved into position. Lance settled into the pilot's seat, slid the shatter-proof enclosure shut, and brought the Skybolt to gurgling life. Lance taxied the plane into position and sent it bustling down the bumpy runway.

As soon as they were in the air, Lance steered the Skybolt out ahead of the still forming flock of birds.

"We need to get ahead of them, then try to disperse them as best we can," Lance shouted over the Skybolt's intercom system. "That's the only way to spare Sarrayota and give us a free shot at Grissom."

"But the birds," Buck cried out, "if even one gets into our propeller..."

He trailed off. Lance knew well the dangers this maneuver posed, but he saw no other alternative. Grissom—the Bird Man—was undoubtedly holding up the rear, and flying around the immense flock storming toward them would take too long and would not prevent destruction being wrought on the poor citizens of Sarrayota. No, despite the risk, this was the only option.

Now with the gigantic mass of birds looming ever closer, Lance maintained his course, aiming the Skybolt straight for them. He clenched his jaw in determination. It was now or never. He reached down to his weapons controls on either side of his seat. From troughs along each engine, two .50 caliber guns peeped out. The telescopic sight dropped down before Lance's eyes, and he fired indiscriminately. Hot lead poured from each gun, as Lance shot down anything that came within his path. The morning sky was filled with the reverberation of the epic battle between man and beast, the cacophony of gunfire obscuring the undoubted squawks and screeches of the hapless animals.

As Lance had hoped, the slaughter and carnage caused the birds to scatter from their original path, frantically fleeing the approaching death. However, their numbers were too high, their mass too dense. The birds battered against the exterior of the Skybolt, but thankfully thus far avoided the plane's propeller. Lance continued the plane's course, firing the twin guns like a man possessed.

"It's working," Buck called out. "They're scattering, no longer heading for Sarrayota."

"But the birds... if even one gets into our propeller..."

Lance allowed himself a brief moment to smile, but he knew the job was only half done; there were still more birds to deal with before...

His thoughts were violently disrupted as a bird, possibly more, smashed into the Skybolt's propeller, causing the plane to sputter ferociously. Could this be the end? To fail before seeing the job through? No, it can't end this way. Lance managed to keep the plane under shuddering control. Was the propeller not as damaged as I thought?

Suddenly, the Skybolt broke through the mass of birds, finally flying into free sky. Still sputtering, Lance was able to miraculously keep the plane aloft. He wondered for just how long..

"Look," Lance said. There, up ahead, was the insidious Bird Man, hovering ominously.

"Can we keep this heap in the air?" Buck called out.

Heap? The Skybolt? But Lance, deep down, wondered the same. He prayed they could keep it together just long enough to deal with the incredible evil before them.

The Bird Man swooped toward them in looping arcs. Lance fired his twin guns, but Grissom was too fast, too agile. The control the villain exerted in the air was phenomenal.

Without warning, Lance jerked the controls, turning the Skybolt around as quickly and as suddenly as he could, and headed back for Sarrayota.

"Get ready, this will take pinpoint timing," Lance ordered.

Lance kept a tight watch on his radar panel, lauded as the most intricate such system in the country, and watched as the Bird Man— as expected—followed. He well knew the incredible speed Grissom was capable of, knew the villain would be upon them swiftly. He watched and waited. At just the right moment, he shrieked, "Now!"

He could hear Buck struggling with the apparatus. He could only hope Buck was able to activate it in time.

"Done," Buck announced.

The Skybolt's controls became harder to manage. The propeller was beginning to shake loose. The plane wouldn't stay aloft much longer. Lance studied the radar panel, gripping the stick with all his might as he did so. He grunted with the strain, peeked at the radar once more. There was no sign of the Bird Man. But, of more pressing concern, was the state of the Skybolt. Lance couldn't keep her flying any longer. The propeller finally slowed, then came to a halt with a sputtering of gears as the engine froze up.

"Hang on, we're going down!" Lance yelled.

"You've got to avoid that lake below us," Buck warned.

Lance was sweating with exertion. The Skybolt was able to glide somewhat without its engines operative, but not for long. Eventually they would either have to bail out, or risk a crash landing. Lance strained to view out of the cockpit, examining the landscape to best determine their next course of action. They'd crossed the expanse of the lake, were now cresting mere farmland, but there were knolls and gullies—often forested—farm houses and telegraph poles. Lance thought it over quickly, decided abandoning ship the best, safest option while they were still high enough in the air.

"We have to bail out," Lance shouted above the sounds of the whipping wind. "Get ready!"

Lance reached down and pulled a lever. In an instant, the canopy shot up, separating from the Skybolt with a large gushing of gas powered mini-jets. In the blink of an eye, both Lance and Buck's seats were ejected, firing into the stratosphere on gas-powered jets, before their parachutes unfurled from the rear of their seats, allowing Lance and Buck to float their way down to safety.

The wind thrashed Lance's face, as he turned his head around frantically hoping to spot the Bird Man but the sky around them was empty. That the winged fiend had not appeared to finish them off as they descended helplessly could only mean Lance's anti-magnetic pulse had done its job. The Bird Man was gone...to his doom, Lance silently prayed.

He strained to see the Skybolt now plummeting into a nearby hill, exploding in a hellish inferno. As soon as they landed, in a field of browning grassland, Lance released himself from his seat, and helped Buck to do likewise.

"'tis a shame," Buck said, eyeing the burning wreckage of the Skybolt in the distance.

Lance remained silent. Yes, his beloved Skybolt was lost, but more importantly, a great evil had been defeated, and untold lives saved as a result. He smiled. In the end, saving innocent lives was all that mattered, was, indeed, worth any risk. He patted his friend on the shoulder, and they began the lengthy walk back to town.

Chapter 8

Lance, Buck and Sheriff Majors congregated at the site of Grissom's burnt out shack. The sheriff scratched his head as he sifted through the rubble, with Lance and Buck watching on.

"It's a complete shambles, nothing can be saved," the sheriff said.

"That's what Grissom intended, to kill me and destroy any evidence of his intentions," Lance explained.

"But how did he manage to control those birds?" Buck asked, concerned that his question, posed earlier, still hadn't been answered.

"That looks to be a secret Grissom's taken to his grave," Lance said, as he raised an eyebrow at the sheriff.

"You were right above Lake MacGonnagle when Grissom fell. We've dredged the lake, but so far no sign of his body," the sheriff revealed.

Lance kicked a piece of burnt-out timber in frustration. "Well, we're done here, sheriff," he said a moment later.

He and Buck turned to head to their bungalow to collect their belongings.

"Lance," Sheriff Majors called out. "Thanks...I don't know what this town would have done without you."

Lance smiled at that, and waved at the sheriff. He looked about the small town of Sarrayota as he and Buck made their way to their rented lodgings. People were milling about, once again going about their day-to-day business without a care in the world. Lance smiled again. His gut instinct to come here had proven to be the right decision, and reinforced to him what his life was about—to use his talents to help people. He knew then what he had to do...

* * * * *

A stark breeze curled through the leafy surrounds of the Long Island cemetery, but Lance gave it no thought. Clean-shaven again, he trudged through the immaculate lawns, a gorgeous bouquet of flowers in his arms, before settling by a large, marble headstone, which bore the words Skip Terrel, A Hero Never Forgotten, Rest in Peace.

Lance lay the bouquet down gently on the lawn, stood straight and removed his sunglasses. A great sadness came over him then, but also a level of determination he hadn't felt for months. He sighed, smiled wanly and briefly.

"I'm sorry kid," he said finally.

The snapping of a branch jolted Lance from his thoughts. He turned. There were his teammates—Buck, Red Davis, James Nolan and Kevin McDouglas. Buck carried another, smaller bouquet of flowers, which he laid beside Lance's on the lawn.

"We thought we'd find you here," Buck said.

Lance managed another wan smile, still felt the emotion of the moment but recognized his friend's heartfelt intentions. After a few more moments of silence, he strode through his team. "C'mon...we have work to do."

The team followed briskly, eager to discover what new adventures awaited them.

THE END

Frank Dirscherl was born in 1973 and has been working as a librarian since 1992. As well as being a writer, he is also a comic book lecturer, amateur history buff and publisher of Trinity Comics, where he writes the multi-Ledger nominated The Wraith comic book series. His other works, *The Wraith* (filmed in 2005), *Valley of Evil, Cult of the Damned* and the non-fiction *The Wraith: Eyes of Judgment - The Official Script Book & Movie Guide*, were all published by Coscom Entertainment. He's also contributed to a variety of pulp anthologies and edited a non-fiction book on independent filmmaking. He lives on the south coast of NSW, Australia with his wife Jennifer, where he's currently working on his fourth Wraith novel amongst other works of fiction. For more information on Frank and The Wraith, please visit www.frankdirscherl.com and www.the-wraith.com.

Lance Star and Me

"Lance Star? I've never heard of this guy!" That was my first reaction when asked to contribute to this new pulp anthology series. I was thrilled at being given such a wonderful opportunity, of course, but while I was very familiar with such pulp characters as the Shadow, Doc Savage and especially the Spider (my personal favorite), I had no idea who Lance Star was, and I wondered if my style of writing was suited to this cheery, heroic aviator. I've been a lifelong fan of such gritty nighttime avengers such as Batman and the aforementioned Spider, so my style of writing has really been tailored to those sensibilities, most notably in my work on The Wraith series of comics and novels. Hence, I worried at whether I could do the kind of story that would please my editor/publisher, but would also please myself. I don't please easily. I needn't have worried, though. With some fine words of encouragement from Mr Fortier (thank you, Ron), I dived in readily, and "Attack of the Bird Man" was the result. In the end, I'm actually quite pleased with it. I hope all of you are as well.

In doing some research on the characters and their world, I found that while there wasn't a lot to be found on the internet, what there was pretty solid, giving me the core, the foundation to be able to build a story upon. This I did. Due to my often incredibly hectic work schedule (often putting in 12-16 hour days—4 of which are spent traveling by train—at a public library, plus working on my own writing projects on the side), some of my colleagues in this anthology ended up doing far more research than I was able to do on my own. For this I am eternally grateful. To them, all of them, as well as to my wife Jennifer, this story is dedicated.

In the end, I'm extremely grateful I agreed to this assignment, for had I turned it down, I would have lost out on working with an amazing group of creators, learning so much from them, and from being able to write about such a wonderful, rich character. It's not often a writer, particularly a writer still in the infancy of their career such as myself, gets such an opportunity to write for characters the like of Lance Star. Despite some initial misgivings, I grabbed this opportunity, and I'm so glad I did. It was a blast, gentlemen. I look forward to the next one.

✈ Lance Star ✈

Where the Sea Meets The Sky

by
Bobby Nash

I - Blindsided

Lance Star did not see the attack coming until it was too late.

The first punch startled him. Catching him by surprise, the hit caused him to lose his precious balance. Before he could regain his footing, a second blow caught him just under the chin. That shot sent him flying over the wooden chairs and onto the old wobbly table.

The table was old, worn out from years of abuse and usage. It was not strong enough to support the added weight of the pilot and its legs gave way under impact, dropping Lance to the floor along with the contents of the table.

Stunned, Lance hit the floor one second before the rain of assorted mixed nuts and lukewarm beer splattered across him.

Lance was on his feet in an instant. "Who the hell hit me?" he demanded, although a quick glance around the room provided the answer.

Not far away stood a lumbering mountain of a man named Niles Isburgh. No longer concerned with the stunned air ace, he was now laughing heartily with his friends, presumably at Lance's expense. Swilling beer and telling tall tales rounded out his activities. He had already turned his back on Lance. He was the only one in the place that was not watching the scene with some perverse satisfaction. That certainly moved him to the top of Lance's list of suspects.

That and the fact that there was no love lost between the two pilots. This was not their first tussle and somehow, Lance suspected, it would not be their last.

Normally when their paths crossed, Lance gave the ill-tempered

That shot sent him flying over the wooden chairs
and onto the old wobbly table.

bruiser a wide berth. Not that the man's size or strength intimidated Lance, but sometimes putting up with another pilot's ego was not worth the effort.

That was a given in Ice's case.

Usually.

But not today.

Enough is enough!

"Ice!" Lance shouted. "You'd better have a damned good reason for this!"

Isburgh turned and wiped drink and crumbs from his thick, matted beard with the back of his hand. People had been calling him *Ice* since he was a teenager because of his last name. However, the moniker became widely used once his hair turned pure white.

When Ice saw the anger burning in Lance's eyes, he could not help but let loose another belly laugh. These two men had never really liked one another. Isburgh thought Lance was a pretentious, glory-seeking showoff.

Lance simply thought Ice was an ass.

"Well, well, well," Ice sneered. "If it ain't the *Air Ace* himself, Lance Star!" He drew out the "L" like an air show announcer might. Another round of laughter filled the room as Ice's cohorts joined in with their leader. "What brings ye to my slice of the world, Lancey Boy?"

"I am in no mood for this, Ice. I'm just in town to see some old friends, take in a little sun, and shake down my new plane. I've got no beef with you."

"Yeah, right," Ice said as he downed another gulp. "Don't presume t' lie to me, Lancey Boy. I know exactly why you're here."

"Care to enlighten me," Lance said as he rubbed his aching jaw. Ice hit like a prizefighter. "Because you seem to know a hell of a lot more about it than I do."

"Don't kid a kidder, Lancey Boy. You're here for the treasure just like the rest of us, ain't ye?"

"Treasure?" Lance was confused. "What the hell are you talking about?"

"Okay, so we're going t' play it that way, are we?"

Lance stood his ground. "I really have no idea what you're talking about, Ice. I promise."

"I don't believe you."

"That's your problem," Lance said. "You're drunk so I'm willing to let bygones be bygones here if…"

"I'm not!" Ice interrupted as he took another swing at the ace pilot from the mainland.

This time, however, Lance was ready for him. He easily sidestepped the big man's clumsy punch. Impeded by drink, Isburgh was no match for his more agile, and sober, opponent. He would not get the chance to sucker punch him as he had before.

Lance used the man's own momentum against him and helped him to the floor.

"Stay down, Ice," Lance said as he rested a boot on his attacker's back.

Before Ice could mutter a reply, his friends took a step toward Lance, who steeled himself for a fight. Suddenly, he wished he'd brought either Buck or Red with him. A wingman would have come in handy at the moment, considering the odds. He had a gun tucked into a shoulder holster under his flight jacket, but knew that pulling it would elevate this from a simple bar squabble into something a lot worse so he decided against that option quickly.

Fortunately for Lance, one step was all they were going to get.

From nearby someone cleared his throat loudly, a subtle way of asking what was going on without actually saying the words. "Am I interrupting something?" Andrew Stewart asked from the bar.

Lance's eye lit up at the sight of the newcomer. "Drew!" he called happily. It was a rare thing for a man in a bar fight would be thrilled to see the local constabulary walk in. Then again, Lance Star was not your average man.

And he had just flown across the Pacific to see the man after all.

"In town less than an hour and already causing trouble, eh Lance?"

"What can I say? These things happen."

"To you, maybe." Commander Andrew Stewart of the United States Navy said as he pointed at the man lying on the floor. "Would you mind letting him up?" he asked, twitching the finger he had pointed at the clearly irritated Isburgh.

"Hmm? Oh, right," Lance said playfully, as if he had forgotten the inebriated treasure hunter was down there. He removed his foot and allowed the big man the chance to get to his feet. He offered a hand to help, but Ice would not accept it.

Drew nodded toward the man who had entered with him. "You guys want me to have the Lieutenant Keyona here take you guys downtown or would you rather just shake on it and call it a day?" he asked.

Lance, offering an olive branch, stuck out a hand.

Reluctantly, Ice shook it tightly.

"Much better," Stewart said as he pointed toward Lance. "What say you and I take a walk."

"Sounds like a mighty fine idea," Lance chuckled.

Drew looked to the pilot he had just rescued. "Ice," he said.

Isburgh nodded and simply said, "Drew."

Moments later, Lance and Andrew were walking along the beach, staring out at the most beautiful sunset either man had ever seen.

"Now there's a sight," Lance said as he marveled at the brilliant washes of red, orange, and purple that filled the crystal clear dusk sky. "There's just something about sunsets in paradise," he said with a smile. "Welcome to Hawaii, Lance. I'm glad you could make it."

II - The Nessie

Sunrise was as stunning as the sunset had been.

Lance woke early and despite the pain in his jaw, made his way to the beach for breakfast and a chance to watch the sun come up over the islands. It had been years since his last trip to the South Pacific and even longer between visits with Drew. He wanted to make the most of both.

Drew, Commander Andrew Stewart, was career Navy. In his hey day he had been one of their top pilots, if not the top. Lance was pleased to hear that time had not slowed his friend, who still flew missions and served as flight trainer for the new recruits. They had met when the Navy had invited Lance and his squadron to come out and run drills with some of their pilots. Lance and Drew became fast friends and had managed to stay in touch over the years.

Last night, after watching the sun go down, the two made their way to a restaurant near the beach and spent hours catching up on old times. They told thrilling tales of adventure and woe, talked of battles and strategies, ate way too much food, and saluted those who had fallen. In their respective lines of work, both men had buried more friends than either cared to count.

The evening ended with the only toast Lance had ever heard his friend utter. "Until we meet again where the sea meets the sky," he said, raising his glass.

Lance laughed after repeating the toast. "At least you're consistent," he told his friend as they exited the restaurant.

The morning air was brisk as the wind blew in off the water. Still, it was warmer in Hawaii than back home in Long Island, New York where there was undoubtedly snow on the ground on this January morning.

"Not the kind of winter weather you're used to, is it?" Drew asked as he walked up to the table, briefcase in hand. Just as he had been the night before, Drew was in his dress whites whereas Lance was wearing baggy civilian attire. They definitely made the odd couple.

"No, sir," Lance answered as he stood and shook hands with his friend. "It's hard to believe that Christmas was just a few weeks ago. Glad you could make it."

"What, and miss out on more of your tall tales? Never."

"My tales may be tall, but I assure everyone of them is absolutely true."

"If not slightly embellished, eh?" Drew chided.

"Don't tell anyone, okay?"

"Your secret's safe with me, my friend." He laughed as he took a seat across from Lance.

Lance sipped his coffee. "So, is this the part where you tell me why it is you called me to Hawaii?"

"I have to have a reason?"

Lance's expression of disbelief was answer enough. "What's going on, Drew?"

"I've got something that's right up your alley, Lance."

"Do tell."

"As you know, the Navy flies test runs out of Pearl Harbor all the time. I run most of the new recruits through just about every battle drill imaginable. Well, a few weeks back one of our dive teams discovered the wreckage of what we've determined is a ship at the bottom of the Pacific, buried pretty deep."

"How deep?" Lance asked, scooping eggs into his mouth.

"Too deep. The Navy and the Honolulu Historical Society have teams all over the wreckage. It's a difficult mission, but our people are up to the task."

"And where do me and my plane come in?"

Drew smiled. "When your last letter mentioned your new plane, I just knew you could help."

"Don't you have seaplanes?"

"Sure, we've been using seaplanes for about twenty years," Drew said as he plucked a piece of bacon from Lance's plate. "But they are small and have no way to transport large groups. Plus, if I know you, she'll also be able to fight if need be."

"Two for two," Lance said. "My plane is larger than your average seaplane. And I don't fly anywhere unarmed. What do you need?"

"Can you really perform water landings and takeoffs in a plane that size?"

Lance's grin spread from ear to ear. "You bet. The Skybolt has a similar function. She can go from monoplane to sesquiplane rather easily. The Nessie takes the same basic principles and expands on them. The best part is the airlock, which is where she differs from the Skybolt."

"Well, there can only be one Skybolt," Drew quipped.

"Too true," Lance agreed. "Although, I should mention that I have not field tested the Nessie on the open seas yet."

"Until now?"

Lance smiled as he popped the last piece of bacon into his mouth. "No time like the present," he said.

*****

Lance Star's heart beat in time to the engine of his newest plane.

He and Drew had taken a Naval staff car to the small hanger Lance had rented to park his new bird while on the islands. "She's a beaut," Drew yelled over the noise as he ran his hands along the plane's outer hull. He noted the lack of a proper paintjob.

"She's still a work in process, I'm afraid," Lance said as he pulled the hatch closed once his passenger was securely fastened into his seat. "I haven't even given her a proper christening yet."

"What do you call her?"

"We're still debating on that one," Lance said. "Until we nail something down we've been calling her *The Nessie*."

"After the Loch Ness Monster?" "

"Like Nessie, this bird glides across the water."

"You ready for a test run?"

"You bet. I've got clearance for you to land at the Naval Airstrip at Pearl. Not many civvies get that honor."

"I'll make sure it's a soft landing for you then," Lance said as he nudged the stick. The Nessie ambled down the runway and within seconds they were airborne, nothing but open sky beneath them.

"I designed Nessie after we had some trouble with a sunken luxury liner a year or so back. Nessie has a lower deck that can be pressurized and used to dispatch rescue divers into the water. She's not as agile as The Skybolt, but I didn't design her for combat so much as for search and rescue."

"Excellent," Drew smiled from the co-pilot's chair. "I'll take a dozen."

"There's only one at the moment, but maybe later on, after this little field test, you, me, and the Navy can work something out."

"It's a deal."

III · Rain of Fire

Dennis Tanaka was growing impatient.

When the call had come in that the Navy had found what they believed to be a sunken ship that could have possibly been built and sailed by ancient Hawaiians, Tanaka and his team of oceanographers and salvagers rushed to the scene. Since then they had done little more than sit and wait.

The United States Navy had its own way of doing things. Sadly, those were not the same way the over eager Tanaka and his colleagues did them. For one thing, they were much slower, more meticulous.

"This is ridiculous," he said for the third time in fifteen minutes. It was becoming his new mantra. His partners were growing tired of hearing it.

"Give it a rest," Dennis," Gail Patterson said. "Just enjoy the sun and sea air. That boat's not going anywhere."

"Patterson was on loan to Tanaka's team from The States. Apparently, someone in Washington DC had taken an interest in the story when the word *treasure* had been used. Tanaka was not happy to have her there and had been quite vocal on the matter, even after his employers overruled his objections. Tanaka did not feel she added anything useful to the expedition. Since they had arrived on site, all she had done was lie around on the bow in a bikini and work on her tan.

The rest of Tanaka's team were hard at work researching vessels reported lost at sea and charting the area using topography maps they pulled from the campus library before leaving for the boat. Lanai Chan was sitting on the floor with several books laid out around her. She was trying to learn everything she could about ancient Hawaiian sailing ships and any conditions that would have sunk the ship. The current thinking was a hurricane or some sort of attack from another ship. Kioni Lau was charting all possible courses that would set the ship into this area. His hope was to backtrack from their present position to the ship's point of origin.

They were not alone in the area. The Navy had a small Cutter moored just off their port bow, although Tanaka preferred the non-military terminology *left* and *right* to *port* and *starboard.* He was more at home on solid ground, a *landlubber.*

The Navy had refused all of his requests to allow divers into the water. They were waiting until they knew exactly what it was they had found before allowing anyone down there. Tanaka had voiced his displeasure at the situation, but his protestations had fallen on deaf ears. *Who are they to tell us where we can and cannot dive?*

Unfortunately, all the boats moving in and out of the area had not gone unnoticed. Soon, word spread throughout the islands of a great treasure having been discovered. Treasure hunters flocked to the area in droves, each eager to stake their claim to the treasures hidden beneath the waves. The Navy was expending a great deal of energy just keeping would be looters away.

All while Tanaka waited impatiently.

"Do you hear that?" Gail asked as she stepped inside the cabin, obviously taking a break from her laborious sunbathing.

"Hear what?" Tanaka asked, exasperation in his voice. Simply talking to this woman frustrated him.

"You don't hear that?" She pulled him out the door and onto the deck.

"What are you...?" Then he heard it. "Planes?" he said skeptically.

"Airplanes?"

Tanaka blew out a breath. "Of course, airplanes." *Can she really be this stupid?* "Sheesh."

"Maybe the Navy sent them to help us?"

"How? Planes don't fly underwater."

"Good point."

"I'm calling it in," Tanaka said as he stepped back inside and picked up the radio receiver.

Unfortunately, he never had time to utter a word. Four fighter planes, each a streaking missile of steel flew toward them at amazing speed. Once they were in range, the planes opened fire, raining a hail of bullets along the hulls of both the chartered boat housing Tanaka and his team and the Navy Cutter.

Neither boat stood a chance.

Tanaka's boat exploded after a hundred bullets shredded the engine, reducing it to floating chunks of fiery debris.

The Cutter was intact, but dead in the water, smoke pouring from its steel frame.

As Dennis Tanaka's lungs filled with water, his last thought as he sank into the cold, inky blackness was a simple one.

At least I'm finally in the water.

IV · The Troops

Lance Star could not believe his eyes.

No matter how often he witnessed carnage, it still hit him like a punch to the gut. Not that he would let anyone see it. He had an adventurous image to uphold after all. It was especially painful when the victims were so young. His thoughts turned back through time to Skip Terrel, a good friend whose life had been cut short far too soon. His death had hit Lance harder than any other pilot he'd ever lost.

Grief over the incident nearly grounded Lance permanently. If not for the support of Buck and the rest of the crew back at Star Field Lance might never have recovered.

Drew had received the call about the attack on the oceanographers and their Navy chaperones shortly after the Nessie touched down at the Pearl Harbor runway.

Moments later, he and Lance were on a boat traveling out to survey the damage.

There were no survivors. The boat leased to the historical society was gone, shred to ribbons by the gunfire. Only small pieces of wood and fiberglass floating on the surface noted their passing. The Navy Cutter was still afloat, but useless. Black pools of oil floated around the boat, obscuring everything beneath the waves.

"Who did this?" Drew asked.

"Could be anybody." Lance said, seeming to think it over. "Hell, you met a bar full of people yesterday with the expertise to pull off something like this."

"Damn," Drew muttered as he stared down at his reflection in the black oil floating all around.

He turned to the nearest officer and issued orders. "I want a full lockdown of this area. No unauthorized vessels in or out of the area."

"Yes, sir."

"And have Pearl put flight crews Alpha and Bravo on standby. I want planes in the air within the hour." He twirled his hand around in a circular pattern, pointing skyward to illustrate his point. Drew had a nasty habit of *talking with his hands.*

"Very good, sir."

Drew turned back to look at the dark water all around them. After a long moment of silence he finally spoke. "Lance, I hate to ask, but…"

"Let me use your radio. I can have them here by tomorrow morning."

"Thank you," Drew said without looking at Lance."

Lance turned and patted his friend on the shoulder before heading into the cabin to use the ship to shore radio.

*****

Buck Tellonger plucked the office phone from its cradle on the second ring. "Star Field," he announced. "Buck speaking."

"Get your feet off my desk, Buck," Lance's voice sounded in his ear, startling his chief of staff. The fact that Lance knew his broad-faced, blue-eyed friend was indeed leaning back in the boss' chair with his feet propped up on the desk was astounding.

"Hey, Lance," Buck nearly shouted as his feet hit concrete. "How's Hawaii?"

"I've run into a little trouble down here," he answered.

"Now there's a shock," Buck joked. His employer had a way of getting himself caught up in some of the most amazing situations. That was part of the reason Buck loved working for Lance Star. Anything could happen.

And quite often did.

"How quickly can you rally the troops and get the Skybolt and a couple Skeeters down here, Buck?"

"We can be wheels up in two, three hours tops."

"Do it," Lance said. "I'll brief you when you get here. The Navy has set aside a hanger for you at Pearl Harbor. Ask for a Commander Andrew Stewart when you arrive."

"I'm on it, Boss," Buck said as he waved through the office window, catching the attention of Eric Davis, whom they nicknamed Red because of his carrot colored hair. Buck motioned Red into the office.

The lumbering redhead did an about face and made a beeline for the office. He opened the door in time to hear Buck finish his conversation.

"Try and stay out of trouble until we get there. We're on the way," he said before hanging up the phone.

"What's up?" Red asked.

Buck stood. "Lance's in trouble. Prep the Skybolt and two Skeeters. Then have one of the field hands make sure the runway is clear and de-iced. I want us airborne in two hours."

"I'm on it," Red said, running back into the hanger to alert the crews to the change in plans.

Buck picked up the phone and connected to the air traffic control tower. "Star Field to Tower."

"Tower," Tony Lamport, Star Field's superintendent of communications responded with his usual heavy Italian accent.

"Tony, this is Buck."

"What can I do for you, Buck?"

"I need clearance for emergency dust off."

"What's the emergency?"

"Lance's in trouble."

"Consider yourself cleared," Tony said before signing off and pulling together clearances.

Less than two hours later, the silver missile that was the Skybolt took off from Star Field, flanked by two Skeeters; one on the left and one on the right. The amphibian Skeeters were smaller in stature and not quite as breathtaking as the spectacular modern marvel that was the Skybolt, but in combat the yellow, black, and scarlet red fighter planes were no less impressive.

Red piloted one of the Skeeters while the big Bostonian, Jim

Nolan took the stick of the second. Buck was behind the controls of the Skybolt, with ex-British flying ace Kevin McDouglas riding second seat.

"Next stop, Hawaii," Buck called over the radio as the planes climbed to cruising altitude.

"Last one there buys the beer," Red called back, trying to lighten the mood.

It helped only a little. They all knew they were mere hours away from a potential battle situation and they had a long flight ahead of them.

Plenty of time to think about their mortality.

V · Black Water

Lance Star carefully steered the Nessie into position.

As he began his descent strong winds blew in from the south, rocking the plane from side to side as her pilot tightened his grip on the stick and maneuvered the finely oiled machine as if it were an extension of his body. The plane dropped slightly through the choppy winds.

Lance looked out his window and gave a thumbs up sign to Drew, who was piloting a Navy bird just off his port side.

Drew returned the thumbs up and Lance toggled the radio mic. Splash down in two minutes," Lance told the divers who were strapped into restraints in the lower compartment. "Make sure you're strapped in, gentlemen. There may be a little chop."

"Roger that," Captain Horne replied as he and his Navy divers readied themselves, verifying that they and their equipment were all securely fastened.

The Nessie flew like a dream under the expert piloting of Lance Star. Lance's reputation was well earned. There was a slight bump as the Nessie touched the water, but Lance quickly smoothed it out as the plane cut through the water as if it were more boat than airplane.

"We're wet, gentlemen," Lance said into the mic. "We'll be at the site in under one minute."

"Roger that. Nice flying, cowboy."

"Thanks, Captain. I'll open the doors on your signal."

Lance eased back on the throttle and brought the Nessie to a stop at the coordinates where he had witnessed the carnage the day before. The first thing Lance noticed was the oil still floating on the surface like a stain on the sea. *Nessie's going to need a good bath*

71

before I take her home.

"Seas getting a little choppy, Captain," Lance called. "I'm in position."

"Open her up, Mr. Star."

Lance cycled open the undercarriage doors.

"I'm seeing a lot of oil on the surface," Lance reported.

"Understood," Horne said. "It seems to be contained to the surface for the moment. We've got a clean entry and my divers are in the water."

"Happy hunting, Captain," Lance said before switching the radio frequency. "Star to Stewart."

"Stewart here."

"Your divers are wet, Drew."

"Very good. We'll continue a flyby up here."

"Understood. Have you heard from my squad?"

"Your chief of staff radioed that they would be here within two hours, Lance."

"Thanks." Lance toggled off the mic and wondered what was keeping his team. He unstrapped himself from the pilot seat and moved into the back cockpit. Unlike fighter planes like the Skybolt, the Nessie was more or less a tricked out cargo plane.

Lance was not normally a patient man. Sitting and waiting for the divers to come back up was not something he looked forward to so he set about keeping himself busy. He checked the wench motor, made sure that everything was in working order. He also rechecked their position on the maps taped up around the small area behind the cockpit.

The rest of the ship was used for air compressors and hydraulics to pressurize the lower deck as well as pumps for emptying the water when the divers returned.

An hour later, Lance was bored. The divers had come back up and exchanged their air tanks and had gone back down. They were having a hard time searching the ship for anything of value. Captain Horne's last report had indicated that his team had found nothing substantial. Certainly nothing worth committing murder for.

They continued searching the murky depths.

*****

Lance heard the planes approaching long before he could see them.

Sitting in the pilot's chair, his head leaned back against the cushioned headrest, he caught the first sound of an incoming plane.

Then he heard another.

And another.

At first he thought it was Buck and the squad, but the sounds were all wrong. Lance had a hand in not only designing his planes, but he had rolled up his sleeves and dug in next to his team to build them too. Lance could pick out one of his birds blindfolded.

He craned his neck so he could get a good look at the sky. Nothing. He could not see the planes, but he knew they were there.

Suddenly, feeling very much like a sitting duck, a rather apt description if he ever heard one, Lance toggled the mic. "Drew, we have incoming. Do you have a visual?"

"I see them, Lance. Too far out for positive ID, but it's definitely not the Skybolt."

"Damn," Lance cursed. "I hate it when I'm right. Should I bring up the divers?"

"Do what you can. We'll cover you."

"Roger that." Lance flipped on the flashing red underwater lights to alert the divers working below of the approaching trouble. Red lights meant trouble and the divers were ordered back to the plane immediately.

"Come on, Buck," Lance whispered. "Where the hell are you?"

Lance reached for the mic again to see if he could reach the Skybolt on short wave and let Buck know the situation. Surely, the Skybolt was close enough to pick up his transmission by now.

Before he could toggle the switch there was an explosion of to the aft of the Nessie. The plane rocked violently under the impact as waves splashed mercilessly against her hull, leaving behind an oily film.

"What the hell?" Lance shouted as he strapped himself in.

That's when he saw the fighters coming in from the east with guns blazing.

And they were heading straight toward the Nessie.

VI · Hornet's Sting

Lance powered up the Nessie's powerful engines.

To save on fuel and to keep the plane steady, he had cut the engines once they were stable. Lance was concerned for the diver's safety while trying to enter and exit the decompression tank with the plane's powerful engines thrumming and churning up the water.

A Lance Star plane had three things you could always count on.

First, they were powerful. There were less than a handful of planes in existence that could touch a plane like the Skybolt in sheer power. While the Nessie was not quite as powerful as Lance's most famous flying machine, she still packed quite the punch.

Second, they were safe. Lance had never lost a plane due to malfunction. While it was true that a few of his birds and some of his best pilots had met an ill-fated demise, it was usually because they were shot down in combat. In the line of duty.

Third, they were armed to the teeth. 'nuff said.

These traits were evident in every plane that rolled out of Star Field. The Nessie was no exception. Lance felt the powerful quivering thrum of the engine reverberate through the steering column. He could hear every vibration.

He liked the sound his planes made. He could sit and listen to that powerfully soothing *thrum, thrum, thrum* for hours on end. The sound soothed him.

He toggled the mic as a hail of bullets littered the Nessie's side, leaving small round impressions in her otherwise smooth hull. "Drew!" Lance shouted into the mic. "We're taking fire down here! Where the hell's my air support?"

"We're on the way, Lance!" Captain Stewart answered. "Just have

*Two of the attacking fighters zeroed in ... and
gave chase... across the waves.*

to take care of something first!"

Lance could hear the tension in his friend's voice. They were in trouble in the air, just as he was on the water. That meant Lance was more than likely on his own.

"No worries, Lance," he muttered to himself as he switched off the light alerting the dive team to return to the plane. "You've been in tougher spots than this. I think."

He switched on another light, orange this time. It was a signal for them to find a place to hole up because there was trouble on the surface. "Time to find a shady spot, guys," Lance said as he adjusted controls and closed the pressure doors and ignited the water pumps.

Unfortunately, the divers could only stay down so long. Within forty-five minute to an hour tops, they were going to start running out of air.

That put a definite timetable on taking care of the newcomers.

That meant Lance needed to be in the air.

"Lance Star to Navy Cutter," he called into the horn. "We're taking fire. Divers are still in the water. I'm going to draw their fire and lead them away. Can you get in there and pick up the divers?"

"We're on our way, Lance," came the static-filled reply."

"Roger that," Lance replied as he jacked the engines to full power. "Star out."

The Nessie cut across the sea like her Scottish namesake, cleaving the waves as if born to them.

Two of the attacking fighters zeroed in on Lance's location and gave chase as the massive seaplane cut across the waves. Bullets pelted the surface of the sea, a few finding their mark and stinging the Nessie's hull like their namesakes.

"Damned Hornets!" Lance shouted as he pulled back on the yoke. Nessie's nose came up out of the water and pointed skyward. Soon, Lance was in the air, which was, as many had speculated, his natural habitat.

Lance banked left as the Hornets opened fire again. This time they missed him completely. "You won't find me quite so easy a target now, fellas."

Lance scanned the skyline, picking out targets and friendlies quickly. "Drew, I'm in the air. Where are…"

Before he could finish the two Hornets circled around and made a beeline for the Nessie again. Lance rolled his bird, easily evading the incoming salvo. He was thankful he had not been able to retrieve the divers before joining the fight. If they had been in the hold he could never have performed that roll maneuver. His passengers would have been tossed around as if they were in an electric dryer.

Lance lined up a Hornet in his sights and opened fire with a burst from the Nessie's gun-ports, showering the fighter plane with the twin mounted .50-caliber guns. He was rewarded by the sight of smoke pouring out of the Hornet's engine as vital fluid lines ruptured and ignited; the plane became little more than a flying brick as it spiraled down toward the waiting waves below.

"One down," Lance muttered, keeping score. "Now where did your partner go?"

As if on cue, the second Hornet came at him from the Nessie's starboard side. The echoing sound of bullets impacting the hull filled the cockpit. Lance winced under the loud clattering sound. It reminded him of the sound Kevin McDouglas' popcorn machine made when popping the kernels.

Lance thrust the yoke forward and put the plane into a nosedive. "Come and get me," he dared the other pilot.

The Hornet's pilot was good. He stayed on Lance's tail, following his dive, his twin guns chattering at the Nessie's aft side.

The water was coming up quick.

Lance set his jaw. *Got to time this just right.*

He jerked the stick and threw the Nessie to port, skimming the seaplane across the waves only inches above splashdown. The plane groaned in protest, but held together as Lance knew she would.

The Hornet was not so lucky. While the pilot had been good, he was no Lance Star. The Hornet hit the ocean waves straight on. At the speed he had been traveling it was akin to flying into a brick wall. The Hornet exploded on impact.

That's two.

Lance pulled back on the stick, taking the Nessie up, up, and away. Circling

Around, he took in an overview of the fight. Drew's squadron consisted of four fighters. Lance noticed that only two of them remained.

And they were outnumbered eight to two.

"Time to even up those odds a bit," Lance said as he put the Nessie on course for the firefight.

"Drew!" he called over the mic. "Hang tight. I'm on the way!"

VII · Sacrifice

C aptain Andrew Stewart was a superb pilot.

Possibly one of the best Lance Star had ever had the pleasure of flying with. And Lance had flown with many of the great ones. Despite his prowess in the cockpit, Lance knew it was only a matter of time before their opponent's numbers got the better of them.

"I'm on your six, Drew," Lance called as he fell into formation behind Drew's fighter plane. Drew plane was smaller and more maneuverable, but the Nessie had more power. Together, they made a lethal combination.

Drew opened fire on the closest bogey, splattering across the Hornet's wing. The damage was minimal, certainly not enough to take the plane out of the fight, but it did slow it down.

Lance swung wide, taking the Nessie in an arc around his wingman's plane and opened up with the .50-calibers, destroying the wing. The Hornet dropped like a stone toward the water.

The pilot leapt out of the doomed plane and Lance watched as his emergency parachute popped open. Angling away from the destroyed remains of his plane, the enemy pilot descended smoothly to the water.

Lance banked left, following Drew as he lined up his next target. Before they could get a bead on the Hornet, the remaining Navy plane exploded as the enemy fighters shredded it with gunfire.

All that remained was Lance and Drew. And they were severely outnumbered.

The Hornets regrouped, circling around in opposite directions in an attempt to box in the pilots.

Lance felt his plane lurch as bullets peppered the Nessie's side.

The Hornets were focusing on the large seaplane. Lance took the Nessie into a dive, the pulled back quickly. The sesquiplane groaned in protest at the undo stress that her pilot was inflicting on her.

Suddenly, Drew's fighter was there, spitting fire at the attacking Hornets.

"Lance," the Navy Captain's voice called over the wireless. "Prepare for a quick port dive. I'll protect your six."

"I'm not leaving you up here alone, Drew!"

The Navy fighter slipped in behind the smoking seaplane, bucking and weaving as enemy fire rained down on them. "No time to argue, Lance! Your bird's got more holes in her than I can count."

"I can hold her."

"Dammit, Star, don't argue! I need you in one piece to get those divers!"

"The divers are covered, Drew. Just stay out of their sites."

Lance angled his plane toward the water below.

Drew's fighter followed.

The Hornets remained in pursuit.

Then, miraculously, Lance heard the three greatest words he had ever heard spoken with a Boston accent. "We're here, Boss!"

The Skybolt came out of nowhere. One second the sky in front of Lance was empty. The next he saw his pride and joy coming straight toward him only to pass by overhead like a rocket. The Skybolt shot toward the Hornets, unloading a massive barrage from the .50-calibers and the 37mm. Automatic engine cannon.

The Hornets, caught off guard, broke off their pursuit.

"Damned fine timing, Jim," Lance called as he fought for control of his wounded beast.

The Hornets split up, breaking formation. The Skeeters gave chase as the Skybolt picked off one of the attacking birds.

Captain Stewart climbed and twisted around for a better look at the odds. Three Hornets were closing on the Nessie. "Who are these guys?" he muttered as he pulled the trigger and opened fire.

Drew dove his fighter to intercept the three Hornets before they could reach Lance's position. The lead Hornet exploded in a fireball that slowed the two following. Drew maneuvered his plane, deftly avoiding the fiery debris as he closed in on the other two planes.

The Hornets opened fire when they saw him approach. He was an easy target. Drew's wing disintegrated, throwing him sideways. Right into the path of the oncoming Hornets. He fought the controls, but his machine had had it.

Collision was imminent.

Suddenly everything was moving in slow motion. The only sound he could hear was his heart beating in his ears.

The Hornets were bearing down on him.

Drew grabbed at ejection control.

The Hornets were so close he could see the flaking paint.

He pulled the ejection handle.

The Hornets hit.

All three planes exploded as one, throwing fire and debris in all directions.

Lance shouted his friend's name, but the voice was lost amid the concussive sound of three gas-powered engines exploding in tandem.

The Nessie shuddered as the prop from one of the Hornets impacted its tail, gouging a massive chasm in the plane's hull. A fatal blow. There was no way the plane could remain aloft.

Lance held his course, fighting the stick every step of the way, even as sparks rained in the cockpit as a fuse blew in the control box just behind the co-pilot's seat, which burst into flames. He eased the yoke forward and set the plane in the water once again, slowing his forward momentum.

"Lance!" It was Buck's voice piping in from the Skybolt. He sounded concerned.

Lance was out of his seat, using the extinguisher to combat the fire. Once the fire was out, he hit the mic toggle. "I'm in one piece, Buck," Lance called. "But they shot me up pretty good. I'm taking on water."

"The rest of the Hornets have turned tail and run."

"Good. One of them bailed. Have the Navy pick him up."

"Will do."

"I'd like to have a word with him."

"Roger that. We're on our way, Boss," Buck said. "Sit tight."

Lance looked around himself at the ankle deep water filling his plane. Angry, he slammed his right fist into his left hand.

"Like I have a choice," he said.

VIII · The Fallen

Lance Star felt numb.

Once again he was sitting at the bar. This time, however, the mood was far from jovial. Everyone had heard of the daring dogfight that had occurred. And they all knew that Drew was dead.

Captain Andrew Stewart had been a fixture in The Air Raid, the local pilot's bar since he had been stationed at Pearl Harbor five years earlier. Many of the Navy pilots hung out at the bar when not on duty. It was also a welcome refuge for those passing through, like Niles Isburgh and his nomadic band of treasure seekers.

Lance was in no mood for conversation and his body language certainly conveyed his thoughts. He, Buck, Red, and the others had come to the bar to toast a fallen comrade.

Naturally, Isburgh made a beeline for Lance and his companions as soon as he walked in the door.

"So," Ice started as he stopped just out of arm's reach. "I'm just here to see an old friend, eh? I don't know nothin' about no treasure, eh? Well, I guess that famous Lance Star reputation for honesty leaves just a bit to be desired, huh?"

"Why don't you shove off, mate," Kevin McDouglas said as he started to rise from his seat. A look and subtle shake of the head from Lance stopped him. Reluctantly, he took his seat.

Ice laughed.

"I am really not in the mood, Ice." Lance did not turn to look at the other pilot.

"Well that's just too bad, Lancey Boy. You see, near as I can figure it, somehow you managed to walk away from all of this while poor ol' Drew didn't. You see, I liked Drew. We didn't always see eye to eye, him an' me, but there was a… what do ya call it, respect there."

"Everybody liked Drew," Lance said as he nursed his drink.

"But not everybody was out there huntin' that treasure, were they?"

Lance got to his feet, spun, and planted a haymaker on Ice, knocking the big man back a step. Lance's pilots were on their feet a second later.

Lance grabbed Ice by the front of his flight jacket. "Was it you?" he shouted into the bearded pilot's face. His rage was palatable. "Did you do this, Ice? Was the thought of treasure so great you couldn't stay away? Or was it the fact that I was out there? Do you really hate me that much, Ice, that you would do this thing?"

Ice pushed Lance away. He stared at him with a hardened contempt. "Let me tell you something right now, Star. When the day comes that I decide to come for you, you'll know it's me. I'll be coming at you straight on. Nothing cowardly like a sneak attack like I heard happened to you today. No, sir. When I come for you, you'll know it."

Before Lance could say another word, Niles Isburgh and his pilots turned and left The Air Raid. He watched them go, wondering for the first time if perhaps he had been wrong about Ice's involvement.

"Well that was fun," Red Davis said as he took his seat.

"Something we should know about, Boss?" Jim Nolan asked.

"Nothing," Lance whispered. "Nothing at all."

Buck lifted his glass. "A toast then. To Drew."

A chorus of "To Drew!" rang from the others, which was quickly echoed throughout the bar.

Lance stood and looked out on the small crowd who had gathered at The Air Raid to pay their respects to a fallen pilot. He held out his glass and repeated Drew's favorite toast.

"Until we meet again where the sea meets the sky."

IX · The Plan

Buck Tellonger was concerned.

As the chief of staff of Star Field, his job was to be concerned. His daily worries included the budget, public relations, bidding on contracts and then negotiating said contracts, and that was before he saw to the needs of the pilots, crew, and their world renowned owner/operator.

Today, however, he was far more concerned for his friend and employer. Both Lance and Buck were seated in the Skybolt, holding altitude at thirty-five thousand feet. Lance was at his usual position at the controls while Buck was handling co-pilot duty.

After the memorial service for Captain Stewart, Lance went into a closed door meeting with some admirals and a few other big muck-a-mucks from the Navy that lasted three and a half hours. When it was all over Lance called the squad together and briefed them on the plan.

The plan was not entirely complex, as master plans go. Still, Buck could not help but feel ill at ease with the situation. Pulling his friend aside, Buck relayed his misgivings. Unfortunately, Lance was not in the mood to listen. And once Lance Star' mind was set, there was no changing it.

That night the Navy moved in a salvage ship and began operations to remove the sunken ship from beneath the waves. Using the cover of darkness, they worked quickly. The next morning, the ship set sail.

Word had been carefully leaked that the sunken ship had been recovered and that, due to safety concerns, the United States Navy was shipping the ship and the contents of its hold to the Naval

Academy at Norfolk, Virginia for analysis and cataloguing.

At 0600 hours, which is six o'clock in the morning for non-military types like Buck, the ship set course for the mainland. Two Navy fighters provided escort for the treasure.

It was all a ruse.

The plan was for the Skybolt, the two Skeeters, and four Navy jets to hold position just within visual range. If everything went according to Lance's plan, the ship with only two escort planes would be too tempting for the scavengers to pass up.

Since it had been Lance's plan, the Navy put him in charge of the squadron. He squelched the mic twice. "Star to squadron. Anything?"

A chorus of negatives came back. There was no sign of the planes that had attacked them before.

"Come on," Lance muttered as he craned his neck for a better view out the cockpit window. "I know you're out there."

Buck picked up the inter-cockpit telephone.

Lance picked up the receiver instantly. "What's on your mind, Buck?" Lance asked. There was no anger in his voice. Lance believed that a man should be true to his convictions. He and Buck were as close as any two brothers. If Buck had issues with the plan, Lance knew he would voice them. And he had.

Lance also knew that a loyal friend such as his chief of staff would watch his six whether he agreed with the plan of not.

"What happens if they don't take the bait, Lance?"

"They will."

"How can you be sure? We put a hurt on them last time. They lost quite a few planes. Maybe we crippled their operation."

"And maybe we didn't. This is the only way to be sure."

Buck paused, contemplated saying more, but decided it would do little good. "Okay, Boss," he finally said.

*****

Eric (the Red) Davis rechecked his instruments.

The Snorter was in perfect working order, but sitting and waiting was not one of his strong points so he did whatever he could to keep himself occupied while he waited.

His thoughts had drifted back to the plane sitting on the slab back at Star Field. Before the emergency take off that brought him to Hawaii, the new plane's thrusters had been giving him some difficulties. There had to be a way to bypass normal flow regulation to accommodate such a strong plane, but so far all of his ideas had come up dry. He knew there was a solution. So far that solution had managed to elude him, but he knew it was only a matter of time until he licked it.

His radio squelched twice, breaking him from his reverie. Then Lance's voice filtered through the radio speaker. "Star to squadron. Anything?"

"Nothing new to report, Boss," he replied after he heard Jim Nolan's Harvard accent report in.

Red hoped that the bad guys took the bait. While he had only met Captain Stewart once before, he had heard Lance talk about him so often that he felt as if he had known him forever.

Red took a glance around the Snorter, scanning the horizon for any sign of the bad guys. If Lance were correct, then they would be coming.

The morning sun had finally crested the top of the islands, throwing a bright incandescent glare across the water. Visibility dropped slightly.

Lance and Buck were watching the ship from the Skybolt while the rest of the planes were keeping an eye out for anyone coming up after the treasure.

Red saw movement below and to the right. He nudged the Snorter into a turn so he could take a better look.

That's when he saw them. Eight small planes flying in formation close to the water. There were also two boats in the water on an intercept course with the salvage ship. Both the planes and the boats were armed to the teeth.

He squelched his mic. "Lance, this is Red. We've got incoming!"

X · Ice Breaker

The enemy planes came in quick.

Lance angled the Skybolt into a descent, angling the flying bullet toward them as they advanced on the decoy vessel.

"Looks like your plan worked," Buck told Lance over the inter-cockpit telephone.

"Was there ever any doubt?"

Buck let Lance's comment go unanswered. Instead he toggled the wireless and radioed the troops. "Buck to all planes. We have incoming. Weapons hot. We're going in."

The Skybolt pulled away from the Skeeters as her pilot poured on the speed.

"Get those cannons ready," he shouted.

"Already on it, Boss."

Lance smiled. His people knew their jobs forward and back. Still, sometimes he felt an uncontrollable urge to remind them that he was still the boss. Plus, he enjoyed giving orders. It made him feel in control.

Something all pilots understood.

The Skybolt moved through the skies like something out of a science fiction movie. Faster than most planes its size, the Skybolt's silver shell glinted in the morning sun, casting a halo effect around it. It was no wonder the Star original had won so many showman awards.

Buck checked the guns. Everything was in perfect working order. Both .50 caliber machine guns were securely mounted at the front of the plane. There was also a 37mm cannon mounted in the Vee off the cylinders. Suffice it to say the Skybolt could pack quite a wallop.

"Warn 'em off, Buck."

Master Gunner Tellonger nudged the trigger and the Skybolt's .50 cals spit fire and a hail of bullets just in front of the approaching planes.

The enemy planes made no attempt to turn away.

"Can't say we didn't warn them," Lance muttered as he toggled the mic. "Safeties off, gentlemen. Plow it up!"

Suddenly, the skies over the Pacific were alive with gunfire as fifteen planes broke formation and went into attack mode.

The Skybolt rocked slightly as two enemy Hornets flew straight at it, spewing lethal stings. Lance deftly maneuvered the sesquiplane, dropping and zagging out of the path of enemy fire.

Buck unleashed a torrent of fire, incinerating one enemy Hornet with ease. The pilot ejected and dropped to the waves below. His emergency chute popped before impact.

The second Hornet was not as lucky.

Buck's aim was dead on. The Hornet exploded in a fireball, spreading scorched debris for miles.

Lance angled the Skybolt around for a run on the incoming boats. Taking a moment to glance at the other planes, he noted that the odds were more or less even. Red's Snorter had been hit and was belching black smoke as he pulled out of the melee and headed for land under a Navy escort.

The Navy pilots were living up to their reputation as well. Unfortunately, Lance caught sight of a Hornet zeroing in on the fighter a scant second too late to help. The Navy plane exploded.

The Hornet peeled off and turned its sights on the Snorter piloted by Jim Nolan.

"Buck! Three O'clock! Dissuade him!"

Several bursts from the Skybolt's cannon were enough to make the pilot chasing the Snorter veer off.

One of the Navy pilots gave chase.

Lance dove his silver bullet toward the ships as Jim's Snorter followed him in. The boat's drivers were far less willing to take on the firepower of the planes as the Hornets had been. The boats turned, arcing away from each other.

The pilot ejected and dropped to the waves below.

"We've got the runner on the left," Lance called as he put the Skybolt on an intercept course. Jim's Snorter and a Navy bird turned off to the right in pursuit of their quarry.

"Where'd those planes go?" Buck asked, scanning the sky.

"There's still two left. Keep your eyes peeled."

Lance opened up with the mounted machine guns at the boat, his bullets hitting frothing the water. "Come on! Come on!" he said between grit teeth as he squeezed the trigger.

The motor sparked as Lance found his aim.

Choking and sputtering, the boat slowed then stopped.

"Gotcha! Dead in the water," Lance said as he picked up the mic. "Navy Cutter, this is Lance Star aboard the Skybolt. We've got a pick up for..."

Before he could finish the remaining two Hornets strafed the Skybolt, their bullets marring the silver streak's shine.

"Where the hell did they come from?"

Buck's voice called out over the phone. "They're coming back around, Lance!"

Lance jerked the stick, taking the Skybolt into a roll even as he heard Buck open fire on the two Hornets. Unfortunately, the Hornet's pilots were smart. Buck could only bear down on one of them at a time. While he concentrated his fire on one plane, the other would target the Skybolt and let loose.

"Where's our backup?"

Jim's chasing down that other boat," Lance answered as another salvo rocked the plane. "This is getting ridiculous."

The Hornets crisscrossed one another's path, drawing fire from the .50 cals. Unfortunately, they were decidedly difficult to hit.

"Looks like they saved the best for last," Buck grunted as he chased one of the planes down only to miss by less than a meter, at best.

"I think we're in trouble!" Buck shouted, unaware that Lance had just muttered the same sentiment from the pilot's chair.

Lance maneuvered again, but the second Hornet had better luck and peppered the Skybolt's hull in a hail of bullets.

Dammit!" Lance shouted.

Buck turned his attention to the second Hornet and fired. This time his luck held and he clipped the Hornet's rudder, sending the plane into an uncontrolled tailspin. "Got him!"

Buck's celebration was short lived as the remaining Hornet opened fire. Bullets sparked off the canopy as Buck instinctively ducked. One bullet found the soft spot and pushed through the thick canopy glass. The bullet tore through Buck's shoulder, passing through before imbedding itself in the seat.

Buck's scream of pain was quickly drowned out by the whistling of air through the newly formed hole in the canopy. His arm useless, Buck could no longer aim and fire the guns.

"Hang tough, Buck," Lance called as he pulled up, hoping to catch the Hornet off guard.

It didn't work.

Lance cursed as his brain scrambled to form a plan.

Suddenly, another plane was there, firing on him. No, wait, not firing at the Skybolt. Lance watched as the streaks of metal passed close by his cockpit and found their mark. That's when he recognized the newcomer.

He dove to avoid more incoming fire.

The Hornet was no match for the incoming plane. Damaged, it limped back toward land.

"Please tell me you aren't here for me," Lance said into the mic.

Boisterous laughter filled his ears. "Not hardly, Lancey Boy," Niles Isburgh said. "I just pulled the famous Lance Star's fat outta the fire. No way am I going to pass up the chance to rub your nose in it for a few years."

"Thanks, Ice," Lance said. "Come on. I've got to get Buck back to Pearl so one of them Navy docs can patch him up. And then…"

"And then what?" Ice answered, suddenly skeptical.

"And then we'll see what we can do about digging up that treasure."

"Sounds like a plan to me, Lancey Boy," Ice said with a laugh as he, Jim, and the Navy pilot all fell into formation with the Skybolt and headed for home.

XI · Interrogation

Lance heard his footsteps echo off the cold stone floor.

Walking down the deserted corridor that lead to the prisoner detention area at Pearl Harbor, neither Lance, his companions, nor their Navy escort uttered a word until they reached the large wrought iron door at the end of the white washed hallway.

"We're here, sir," the escort, Lt. McMennamin said as he opened the door.

Lance Star stepped through first, with a nod to the Lieutenant who had been assigned to him during his visit. Buck Tellonger followed close behind his boss. Niles Isburgh brought up the rear.

Their escort remained in the hallway and stood post at the door.

"Welcome, gentlemen," a Navy Commander said as they entered. Lance remembered being introduced to the man by Drew just two days earlier, but the young man's name escaped him at the moment.

The officer shook each man's hand in turn and introduced himself as Commander Hudziak before motioning them into the room on their left. It was dark inside, save for the large window that looked into another room where a light was burning. It was not the first time Lance had been in an interrogation center.

"You got anything out of him yet?" Lance asked.

"No. He's been fairly tight lipped."

"Can't say I blame him," Isburgh said. "Murder of a Navy officer carries some pretty stiff penalties if I recall correctly."

"Yes they do," the Commander confirmed. "Very stiff."

"I'm still not sure what you need us for?" Buck asked, readjusting his wounded arm in its sling.

"We were hoping you might be able to help us identify him."

Lance looked through the window at the pilot he had shot down. The one who had managed to eject before his Hornet exploded.

"Anyone you know?"

"I do," Isburgh said softly, his words barely more than a hoarse whisper. "His name's Dirk Landress. I've had a couple run-ins with him before. He's something of a mercenary. Fights for whoever pays him."

"I wanna talk to him."

"I assumed you would, Mr. Star," Commander Hudziak said. "I've secured clearance for you."

"Mind if I join you?"

The question caught Lance off guard. "Excuse me?"

Niles Isburgh was not a man unaccustomed to asking for anything. He squared his broad shoulders and looked Lance straight in the eye. "Drew was my friend too," he said. "There are not many men in this world I respect, Star. Drew was near the top of a very short list."

Lance eyed the Commander.

"It's your call, Mr. Star."

Lance sized up Isburgh. "You follow my lead. Understood, Ice?"

Isburgh grinned. "I can be your wingman," he said. "Just this once."

*****

Lance stepped into the room first.

Although they had never met, the prisoner, Dirk Landress looked up at him with contempt in his eyes. His expression turned to surprise when he saw Niles Isburgh step into the room behind Lance Star.

These men could not be more opposite. Yet, the one thing they had in common was Captain Andrew Stewart. That was enough to temporarily suspend their ongoing feud.

"Hello, Dirk," Lance said as he took a seat across the table from him. Ice leaned against the wall near the one way mirror they had been on the other side of moments ago. He crossed his arms over his thick, broad chest, a deep, intimidating scowl on his face.

"I assume you know who we are," Lance continued when Dirk

said nothing. "We're here to talk about who it is that hired you."

Dirk *harumphed.*

"You're facing some very serious charges. You're the only suspect we have in the deaths of several Naval officers and a boat full of scholars from the university. With the state of the world today, the Navy doesn't have time to play games with you."

"Go to hell," Dirk spit.

Lance came out of his chair like a bolt. He grabbed the handcuffed prisoner by the collar and dragged him bodily to his feet. He leaned in close, his voice deep and menacing.

"Now you listen to me you little sonuvabitch," Lance growled. "One of those men you killed was a good, close, personal friend of mine and I'll be damned if I'm going to let the person who ordered it get away with it."

"You don't scare me, Star," he hissed.

Lance let go, allowing the prisoner to drop back into his seat.

Seething, Lance stepped away from the table. It had taken all of his control not to throttle the man.

His eyes locked with Isburgh's. Ice had watched Lance's outburst without comment. Lance nodded at the silent question in Ice's eyes. *Batter up.*

Ice stepped forward and calmly leaned down on the table, resting his fists on the tabletop. He looked straight into the prisoner's eyes. "You might not be afraid of him," Ice began. "But I think you might be of me."

Dirk Landress stammered. "Why are you here with him?" he asked. "I thought you two hated each other?"

Ice smiled as he turned his gaze toward Lance, who was now standing near the mirror. "Well, there's a lot not to like, but you see, Dirk, this ain't about me an' Lancey Boy over there."

"It's not?"

"No," Ice smiled as he stared at the prisoner. "You see, that man you killed that was a friend of his, well he was also a friend of mine. Now, Star is something of a celebrity. That means he has to keep his public image squeaky clean."

Lance felt heat grow in his cheeks, but bit his tongue and let Ice play his hand.

"Now me, on the other hand, I have no such limitations," Ice said.

For the first time, Lance could see fear in the prisoner's eyes.

"I'm sorry," Landress stammered.

Ice smiled at the chained pilot. "Not yet you aren't."

XII · Respects

Lance Star took one last long look at the beautiful sunrise over paradise.

He stood on the dock at Pearl Harbor, watching the morning sunrise over the top of the islands. The water was alive with vibrant colors and glare, gleaming off the ships docked in port. Another beautiful day in paradise was dawning.

The prisoner, Dirk Landress had finally broke. Lance could understand somewhat. Ice was intimidating most of the time, but he could be downright scary when he had to be. That was all it had taken to make the prisoner crack and start talking.

Landress had spilled his guts about the man that hired him. A Hawaiian mobster named Kiani, apparently. Lance had offered to help the Navy with the raid, but they assured him that the situation was under control and that his assistance would not be required.

He almost fought them on it, but then thought better of it. There was something to be said from remaining in the Navy's good graces. Especially since he intended to donate the Nessie to the Navy after her overhaul and a name change to name her after his fallen friend, Drew.

He sensed the man approaching him before he even heard his footfalls on the deck. "Howdy, Ice," he said without turning.

"Star."

"You come to make sure I was actually leaving?"

"Something like that," Ice said with a smile even though Lance had yet to turn around to see it. "There's not enough room for two celebrity pilots on these islands."

"Who else is here?" Lance joked.

Niles Isburgh ignored the jab, stopping beside Lance. Together they looked out at the ocean. "I just wanted to thank you," Ice said. "Commander Hudziak tells me you put in a good word for me and my team to help them with salvage operations."

"Call it a moment of weakness," Lance said. "Don't tell anybody."

"Your secret's safe with me, Lancey Boy."

"And that's another thing," Lance said as he turned on Ice. "I really hate being called that."

Ice smiled before turning to walk away. "I know," he said.

Unable to stop himself, Lance felt a grin tug at the corner of his mouth.

"Catch you up above the clouds, Star."

And then he was gone, leaving Lance alone on the dock to watch the sun rise.

From that day forward, every sunrise would remind him of his friend, Drew Stewart. Just as with his friends that had passed on before, Drew would forever be a part of him.

Just like Matt Hendersen, Jack Falcone, and Skip Terrel.

For the first time in a long time Lance could think about his departed comrades with something other than sadness. Hope. He realized that he would see them all again someday.

"See ya, fellas," he whispered. "In that place where the sea meets the sky.

THE END

Bobby Nash is the writer/artist of the comic strip *Life In The Faster Lane.* Comics written by Bobby include Fuzzy Bunnies From Hell [FYI Comics]; Bubba The Redneck Werewolf [Brass Ball Comics]; Demonslayer, Threshold, and Jungle Fantasy [Avatar Press]; Yin Yang [Arcana Comics - coming 2008]; and Fantastix: Code Red [coming soon]. Bobby's prose work includes his 2005 debut novel, Evil Ways [Publish America] and the 2006 novel Fantastix [Optic Studios/FYI Comics]. Bobby's pulp anthology work includes Lance Star: Sky Ranger [Airship 27 Productions, originally released through Wild Cat Books in 2006 and re-released through Cornerstone Books in 2008]; Startling Stories Magazine 3 [featuring Samaritan - Wild Cat Books]; Sentinels Widescreen Special Edition [short story - White Rocket Books]; and the upcoming Domino Lady [Moonstone Books - July 2008].

For more information on Bobby Nash please visit him on the web at www. myspace.com/bobbynash, www.comicspace.com/bobbynash, www.bobbynash. com, and www.fasterlane.blogspot.com.

Bobby lives in Bethlehem, Georgia.

Where the Fingers Meet the Keyboard

Writing a Lance Star adventure

Lance who?

That was my first reaction when Ron Fortier first asked me to write a tale for this volume back in 2006. With great enthusiasm, our esteemed editor told me a bit about the character and off I went to that magical place where the fingers meet the keyboard.

Let me take this opportunity to introduce you to Lance Star as I know him.

Lance is a man's man. He's rough and tumble, not afraid to get his hands dirty. He's a man who speaks his mind and is very protective of his crew, the Sky Rangers. He would travel the four-corners of the Earth to help any one of them. As they, in turn would for him. I wrote Lance as if portrayed by John Wayne. As heroes go, not a bad place to start.

Lance is a genius. Not only is the man a certified Air Ace, but he also designs and builds his own planes. One of the tasks the writers for this volume were assigned was having a new plane show up in each story. That request led to the creation of the Nessie in my story, "Where The Sea Meets The Sky." I'm not sure if The Nessie would fly in reality, but it sure was interesting to write.

Lance surrounds himself with an excellent crew. Buck Tellonger, Red Davis, James Nolan, Kevin McDouglas, and even those characters that were just out of our reach like Walt Anderson, Jack Falcone, and Skip Terrel. Each was fun to write, even though there were a few I regrettably did not give enough time in the spotlight this go-round. An oversight I plan to make up for in some upcoming Lance Star: Sky Ranger projects.

I would like to thank my fellow writers, Bill, Win, Frank, and Larry, who really turned in some fantastic pulp yarns for this volume, artist Rich Woodall for the really cool illustrations, and Joe Kenworthy (and Rob Davis) for his incredible PhotoShop skills that made the Sky Rangers photo in the back of this volume a reality. I'd also like to thank Ron Fortier and Ron Hanna for getting our first release off the ground and into the air. And finally, thanks to Airship 27's Ron Fortier and Rob Davis, along with Michael Poll at Cornerstone for getting the Sky Rangers back in the air where they belong.

My time in the air corps with Lance Star and his Sky Rangers has certainly been fun. I'm looking forward to dropping by Star Field again and listening to more of Lance Star's amazing adventures.

I hope you'll join me.

Bobby Nash
Bethlehem, GA

Lance Star

Shadows over Kunlun

by
Win Scott Eckert

Early 1941

Lance Star was right where he wanted to be: in the cockpit of the *Silver Skybolt II*, twin Diesels pushing the large, sleek sesquiplane smoothly through night skies toward another rendezvous with adventure. The Skybolt II was a newer version of the best plane he had ever flown. The original had been lost a few years back.

Cruising off his wing at three-hundred mph were two of his best men. Lance's Chief of Staff, "Buck" Tellonger, and Eric "Red" Davis, were flying the speedy Skeeters of Star's design. Both expert pilots were clad in their trademark white helmets. The running lights of the two Skeeters winked at Star reassuringly.

As the three planes approached San Francisco, Star checked the status on the gleaming instrument panel. He reflected on the mysterious summons that had sent the three men speeding westward from their East Coast headquarters.

Just yesterday, he had received a letter, hand-delivered by a motor-cycle courier to Star Field in Long Island. The messenger had strict orders to hand-deliver the message to Star and no one else. Although the man was dressed in civilian clothing, he gave off a distinct military air. The messenger had told Star that he was instructed to wait and carry back the reply.

Lance had replied in the affirmative, and then called up Kevin McDouglas, the old Scotsman who was the majordomo of Star Field.

"Lance! Calling about the tests on the new equipment on the Skybolt II?" McDouglas inquired with his characteristic Scottish burr.

"Never mind that, Kevin," Lance had said, and proceeded to give precise orders, in strictest secrecy, regarding the upcoming departure. Only the head mechanic was to be notified so that their planes could be readied.

Lance would have preferred to let his whole staff in on it. After all, the losses they had suffered in the past few years had brought them even closer together, and they were the only real family that many of them had.

But the communiqué had been clear: only share the details on a need-to-know basis.

And so, twelve short hours later, Lance, Buck, and Red were making their final approach into San Francisco Bay.

⊹

Frisco was in the middle of a real pea-souper, and most of its denizens were curled up at home about the fire or around the radio, listening to their favorite nightly programs.

A few hearty souls, though, and perhaps some of the less savory rats making the rounds at the various waterfront dives and speakeasies, were outside cutting their way through the dank, yellow fog. These were the ones who heard it, a faint buzzing coming from over the water. The buzzing was faint, and yet by a peculiarity owing to the way the sound traveled through the fog, it sounded to those who could hear it at all as if it were right on top of them.

The sound soon evolved from the invisible buzz to a loud whine, and thence to an even louder droning.

One of those aforementioned less than savory characters took an especial interest in the rising noise, and turned toward the water.

The mists shifted and separated briefly, and three large shapes were seen to emerge dramatically from the low-hanging fog and blaze under the Golden Gate Bridge. The three shapes resolved themselves into the sleek Skybolt and Skeeters. The planes skimmed onto the water in a cool, expert landing, and taxied in toward the waterfront.

The watcher slipped deeper into shadows and observed as Star and his men tied up the planes at a dockside warehouse labeled Hidalgo Trading Co. The Hidalgo was owned by a friend of his back in New York, and had warehouses at several major ports. Lance's planes would be well-tended.

As Lance, Buck, and Red made their final arrangements at the docks, the hidden spectator continued to monitor them from the shadows of the dark, decrepit warehouse which adjoined the Hidalgo Trading Co.'s facilities.

Their aircraft in good hands, the three pilots hailed a cab and piled in, exhausted.

As the taxi sped off, the watcher moved out of cover of the darkened warehouse and blended into the deepening fog. There was a strange whistling, almost like a bird hooting, and then he was gone.

✛

Lance, Red, and Buck were settled into a suite on the ninth floor of the Belmont Arms Hotel. They had ordered a pitcher of hot coffee and devoured three T-bones, and were now regrouping and taking stock of the situation.

"So Lance, what's it all about?" Red asked. "You hustled us out here so quickly, we didn't even have a chance to find out."

"It must be something important. You wouldn't even fill us in over the radio on the flight out," Buck said.

"That's right, it is important, and I think you two will find it very interesting. I received a letter from a government man named Lee. Apparently some big shot in Chinatown here. Anyway, he asked us to come out as soon as we could. He specifically asked for you two."

"Us," Red exclaimed. "What does the government want with us?"

"I think you'll be quite intrigued. Here, read the note from Lee." Lance pulled a sheet of paper out of his coat pocket and handed it over to Buck and Red.

Mr. Star [the note read]:

I hope you will forgive the rather abrupt nature of this missive's delivery, but it is most essential that I consult with you quickly on a matter of tremendous importance to our government.

A gentleman of my acquaintance recently returned from the Far East. This man is a businessman, completely loyal to our country and yet able to move about Asia in the highest circles of influence with the greatest of facility. He brought me much interesting news upon his return, but only one item which is of concern to you.

I ask you now to recollect what may seem like ancient history. During the Great War, there was a famous American ace known as "Le Faucon Rouge." Le Faucon operated as an outlaw, and apparently no one knew his real identity, which does make it odd that he was known to be American.

In any event, Le Faucon Rouge, as you no doubt recall, disappeared without a trace after the War. Many have speculated that, having played his part in the conflict, he quietly retired to a civilian life in America.

My businessman acquaintance has news to the contrary. Indeed, he brings news of Le Faucon Rouge from Tibet, of all places.

If you would be so kind as to come to San Francisco, post haste, I would like to discuss with you my proposal for a small expedition to Tibet, to be led by you, for the purpose of locating this American hero and bringing him safely home, where he will receive a full pardon.

I believe that your associates, Tellonger and Davis, will have reason to be interested in news of Le Faucon, and I urge you to bring them.

Beyond that, please do not share the purpose of your trip or your destination with anyone else, save those of your staff it is absolutely necessary to inform. This information may impinge on matters of national security, and I urge you to consider it in that regard.

My messenger awaits your immediate reply.

Very truly yours,

Lee

"Polite, isn't he," Buck said.

"Yeah, but it's what he doesn't say that's got me on needles!" Red said. "Le Faucon Rouge! If Lee knows just where he is and what happened to him after the War, why doesn't he say so?"

"I think that's why he called us out here," Lance said.

"Well, when do we get to meet this Lee, anyway?" Red asked. "If he's got info on Le Faucon, I want to know now!"

Buck and Red had flown Spads, Nieuports, and S.E.5s. together in France during the Great War. They had saved each others' lives on more occasions than they could count, and were closer than brothers.

But both men were clearly in shock about the news of the legendary Le Faucon Rouge.

"Lee should be in touch soon," Lance said. "Why don't you tell me more about Le Faucon? You both seem pretty worked up."

"Lance," Buck replied, "you've heard us go on and on about all the dogfights we were in. All the times Red and I pulled each other's fat out of the fire."

Lance nodded.

"Well," Buck continued, "Le Faucon also saved our tails more times than we can count, appearing out of nowhere. And not just us. Ask half the boys who flew out of France. He probably appeared just in the nick of time for at least half of them. He was a one-man squadron!"

"What else do you know about him?"

Red chimed in. "Well, there were rumors that Le Faucon was an American flyer who had been framed in the past by his own pals. There were other tales: his aide was a giant African named Akis; he had escaped a firing squad to hide out in an aerie high in the rugged Vosges Mountains and fight his own aerial war against war; and so on. I heard he had almost been pardoned once, but it didn't take and Le Faucon escaped once more to continue his own war."

"Lee says he disappeared without a trace after the War ended," Lance said. "Was there ever any scuttlebutt on what happened?"

Red looked abashed. "I guess I never really thought about it. I assumed he went back to the States and got on with his life."

"With a crime hanging over him?"

"Yeah," Buck added, "it doesn't make sense, does it? I mean, if Le Faucon was once summoned to receive a pardon, that means that *someone* high up knew his real identity. Which means... he couldn't go home after the War."

"That isn't right," Red said. "Le Faucon saved all those lives. He probably even turned the tide once or twice. He was a hero! I can't believe that he was ever guilty of any crimes!"

"Well," Lance said, "Lee's summons does label him a hero. Perhaps the government is willing to finally pardon him and welcome him home. If so, we can only hope that this news of him in Tibet is accur—"

A series of loud hoots and whistles came from outside the French doors of their suite.

"What is that, some kind of bird?" Red asked.

"Couldn't be anything else, we're nine floors up and that balcony is damn small," Lance rejoined.

Before any of the men could utter another word, the glass doors came crashing in, followed by three small dark shapes and the roiling fog.

"What the hell—?" Buck choked out, and then the time for words was over.

A small brown man leapt at Buck, a length of cord wrapped tightly around the fingers of both hands. In seconds, the cord whipped around Buck's throat, although he just barely managed to slip his right hand up between the cord and the soft flesh of his neck. The small man was perched atop Buck's shoulders and tightened his grip.

Buck fell to his knees, gasping for breath.

Meanwhile, Red was under siege from another man who came at him with a flurry of hands and feet. The man moved so fast that Red could barely block effectively, and went down under a hurricane of blows.

On the other side of the room, the third small man had Lance at bay with a long, wavy knife. Lance's only defense was a wood-framed chair which he held in front of him, like a lion-tamer fending off his angry charge.

Without any visible movement on the small man's part, the dagger seemed to magically flit through the air. Before Lance could even react, the greater length of the blade had split the chair cushion before the razor sharp tip came to a halt a few inches from Lance's torso.

LANCE'S only defense was a wood-framed chair which he held in front of him...

He looked down at the knife which had come so close to perforating him, and then quickly looked up again. Two more wavy daggers were in his opponent's hands, ready to fly.

"Guys, a little help here?"

"Love to... Lance... but I'm a little tied up here," Buck grated out. His face was turned an ungodly shade of blue.

With what was clearly a final, desperate gambit, Buck got his legs under him and thrust upward and backward, in the direction of the balcony. The two men propelled backward through the broken glass and debris, straight toward the wrought iron railing. At the last possible minute, Buck bent his legs, lowering his center of gravity. The momentum continued to carry both men backward and the small man's spine bore the brunt of the impact against the top of the railing.

There was a sickening crunch, and the cord about Buck's throat immediately loosened. He fell to the concrete floor of the balcony, gasping for blessed, life-giving air. It was thick with fog, but he'd take it.

The other man wasn't so lucky. A line of blood trickled from his mouth and his dead eyes stared glassily into the night.

Buck struggled to his feet and made his way back inside to see how his compatriots were faring. But before he got one step inside, a knife came flying from Lance's opponent. It flew through Buck's sleeve and embedded in the frame of the late French doors, effectively pinning Buck like a fly.

Red had fared a little better, but finally planted a lucky left hook. For all his opponent's flying kicks and chops, he had a glass jaw and went out like a light—but not before landing a last, solid kick to the face which knocked Red for a loop. The room spun and Red fell to the floor, unconscious.

"C'mon guys," Lance said. "This chair is starting to resemble a good hunk of Swiss cheese. It won't last forever, and I don't have anything else to offer up against our knife-wielding friend."

"I'm trying, Lance," Buck yelled. "He pinned me, but I should be free in a second."

Another dagger penetrated the chair, Lance barely blocking the flying blade in time.

"One more second is all it's going to take! Where's Red?"

"He's lying on the floor behind you. He looks knocked out, but his guy is out of it too!"

Yet another knife whistled toward Lance, hurled with such strength that when it was blocked with the chair, the force actually knocked Lance on his back. Although he managed to keep the chair from falling on him with full force, the wooden arms cracked loudly as they hit the ground. The chair frame collapsed, sending the cushion—and the multiple blades sticking through it—descending toward Lance's prone form.

The little brown man raised his arm to toss one more dagger for good measure. Another loud crack came, at the same time as Buck freed himself and leapt toward the chair cushion and its deadly set of knives which was descending toward Lance's chest.

Buck knocked the cushion and knives away, his momentum carrying him over Lance, and he rolled onto his feet to confront the deadly knife-thrower. Who lay on the floor, a single neat bullet hole in his chest.

A well-dressed Chinese man stood in the doorway of their hotel suite. The pistol in his hand was still smoking.

Buck made ready to confront this new threat.

"No, Mr. Tellonger. That won't be necessary." The newcomer's voice was low and well-modulated. He picked up one of the daggers. "Ah, a *kris*. I might have known."

Looking up, the stranger put his gun away and addressed Buck again: "Mr. Tellonger, I am on your side."

Lance made it to his feet and stood beside Buck. "Who the hell are you?"

The man removed his black Bowler hat and held it slightly in front of him as he gave a slight bow.

"I am Mr. Lee. At you service." He bowed slightly again.

✥

The police had been called, and Lee had adroitly handled them. The coroner had also come to collect the bodies—all three bodies, as it turned out. The third man, Red's opponent, was also dead.

"These types of men commit suicide. Their fate would be worse than death if they allowed themselves to be captured," Mr. Lee said. He was well-spoken, six feet tall, and Yale-educated.

"What type of men do you mean? And just how did he commit suicide?" Lance asked. The four men were now ensconced in another suite, the pilots' former quarters having been totally demolished in the mêlée.

"They are called 'dacoits.' I think that forensic examination of the body will reveal that the third dacoit ingested some type of herb or plant which caused immediate death. If these men were employed by the one whom I suspect, it would fit his preferred methodology."

"And just who is that, anyway? Mr. Lee, we're here at your mysterious summons, and no sooner than we arrive are we the target for murder. I think it's time you filled us in."

"Of course, Mr. Star. I'll start at the beginning." Lee lit a Red Apple cigarette and settled into a comfortable leather armchair. The other men pulled up similar chairs and settled in. Perhaps they'd finally get to the bottom of this.

"You have all read the note I sent to Mr. Star? Good." Lee puffed at his cigarette, then continued. "Shortly after I sent my message to Mr. Star, my business acquaintance who had recently returned from the Far East—"

"Your agent, you mean. You *do* work for the government?" Lance interjected.

Mr. Lee gave a tiny shrug of agreement. "As you say. My 'agent,' then, was murdered. His body was discovered at the docks. Given the attack on you men this evening, I suspect that the three late dacoits were responsible for his murder."

"Beyond my agent's—let's call him X for convenience. All I have beyond X's original communication to me that Le Faucon Rouge is alive and well in Tibet, is a code which describes a location in Tibet by latitude and longitude. I didn't learn any more from X before he was killed, and there was no indication as to why this information might be worth killing a man over."

"But you must have some idea," Lance said. "Now that there's murder involved, there has to be more to this than a straightforward case of bringing a pardoned man home to a hero's welcome."

"Perhaps you are correct. My Washington contacts indicate to me that before Le Faucon Rouge appeared in the skies of Europe, he was an American military man stationed in Egypt. He apparently stumbled upon something called the 'Midnight Sun.' There are no records as to exactly what Midnight Sun actually was. Immediately thereafter, Le Faucon was charged with treason—the records are not specific as to the crime. He was branded a traitor. However, he escaped within hours of being captured and charged. And thus never had a chance to turn over the key to the Midnight Sun to his superiors."

"Then," Lance said, "he's never been cleared."

"That is correct. However—"

"Le Faucon saved our butts more times that I can count!" Red said. "There's no way I'm bringing him back just to face a government tribunal on some trumped-up charge from more than twenty years ago!"

"I'm with Red on this one," Buck said.

"Gentlemen, gentlemen, please." Lee held up a hand. "The government agrees with you. Le Faucon Rouge will be fully pardoned."

"Even if he no longer has this Midnight Sun, or still won't turn it over?" Lance asked.

"Even so. Ancient secrets are just that. Whatever Midnight Sun was, it is almost twenty-five years out of date. We doubt it can be of any possible value to us now."

"And yet..." Lance said. "Somebody is willing to kill us, and your agent, over this business."

"Let me put it this way," Lee said. "If Midnight Sun *does* still have some kind of value to us, and if Le Faucon is willing or able to turn it over to us, we certainly will not turn him away. But in any event, he is being offered a full pardon and a return home to America."

"Fair enough. I do have several more questions. Since it's known that Le Faucon was formerly stationed in Egypt, you must know his real name," Lance said.

"His true name is Rand, although I doubt that will help you much in the search for him."

"True, but assuming we do find him, it would be nice to address him by his given name. Next: why us?"

"It was decided that a certain kind of men should be sent to investigate X's claim that he had discovered Le Faucon's whereabouts. Since the case involves a flier, the men should be pilots, and used to rough spots. Besides, you can get across the globe faster in your planes than by ship. Also, Tellonger and Davis are among the few men still flying twenty years later, who have any connection at all to Le Faucon Rouge. You and your men fit the bill. Obviously there will be danger, as evidenced by my agent's murder and the attempt on your own lives."

"All right. Final question."

"Go ahead." Lee stubbed out his cigarette and lit another.

"You said you suspected the person behind the dacoit attack on us. Who is it?"

"It pains me to say that it is a countryman of mine. This person has been actively opposed to Western interests for at least thirty years, perhaps more. He claims no other motivations than the mere defense of his homeland against Western imperialism, and yet I believe his ambitions run much deeper than that. For many years he confined his activities to opposing the British, but in recent years brought his crusade to these shores, and even went so far as to attempt to manipulate a recent U.S. presidential campaign."

Mr. Lee seemed to lose some of his cool, collected demeanor, as he continued. "This man is a genius of the highest order, a scientist and a medical doctor. As I've made clear to my superiors, it is this man and the legions at his command—his *Si-Fan*—that we in the West must fear, not China itself."

"I see..." Lance raised his eyebrows somewhat skeptically. "And what is this man's name? Just in case we meet him in a dark alley," he added.

"He won't personally accost you in any dark alleys. He has plenty of trained assassins for that. But you'll ignore my warnings to take this man seriously at your peril—as you've already seen tonight. He is known by several names, such as Shan Ming Fu and Hanoi Shan. But the name I have most often heard whispered of late is Doctor Natas."

Lee crushed out his second cigarette. "So. How about it? Will you go to Tibet and investigate?"

Lance looked at Buck and Red, who nodded silently back at him. "Sure," Lance said. "Why not?"

✝

The three planes, the Skybolt II and two Skeeters, cut a swath through the raging blizzard. The latitude and longitude coordinates provided by Lee marked an area deep in the mountains in Tibet. It was a dangerous, bitter, unexplored area, and Lee had made sure that Lance and his men were outfitted with the latest in cold-weather survival equipment.

Through the long journey across the globe, the men had stopped only briefly for refueling and provisions. During flight, the planes' auto-pilot systems were linked together by a radio-control device of Lance's invention. This meant that each of them could sleep in eight-hour shifts while the other two kept watch. In this way the three adventurous pilots made excellent time.

Now, in the midst of the roiling snowstorm, visibility was nil, and the three planes were also connected to Lance's infra-red telescope via the radio remote control system.

It was also providential that Star's new Skybolt II was outfitted with skis for landing, in addition to the amphibian pontoons. Likewise Buck's and Red's Skeeters had recently been retrofitted with landing skis.

Although, now that Lance thought about it, Lee must have known about the recent retrofits to their aircraft when he contacted Lance. Lee surely knew more than he was saying, about a lot of things. The attack at the Belmont Arms Hotel in Frisco couldn't have been random, and Lee had already identified a suspect—the enigmatic Doctor Natas—so why not just come out and admit that there was still interest in Midnight Sun.

Whatever that was.

Star was shocked back out of his reverie as his instrument displays began to glow brighter and brighter, emitting a white hot light. The control stick became hotter to the touch. He switched on his radio.

"Buck, Red, do you read?"

"I read you, Lance," came Buck's reassuring tones. "But I'm having a bit of a problem here."

"Me too," Red Davis chimed in. "My instruments are *melting*!"

"It's happening here too. Stay calm," Lance said. "We're almost to the coordinates. Reduce airspeed to one-fifty. Anything still working?"

"Radio, obviously, although that's starting to glow and burn up, too. We'd better do our talking fast!" Red said.

"Make sure all gear is in position for snow landing, now, before the hydraulics fail," Lance instructed.

Green floating gear lights blinked on as landing skis folded out of the fuselages and wings of the three great planes.

"Fall back and hone in on my running and tail lights. The infra-red-ray telescope is still functioning. I'm going to take us in. Roger that?"

"Understood, Lance," Buck said.

"I got it!" Red replied.

"Signing off," Lance said.

He switched on the infra-red-ray telescope and aimed it into the swirling blizzard below. The wind howled along the silver fuselage as he brought his fighting ship around into a tight spiral and headed down.

Critical systems continued to glow, melt, and fail, and it was becoming unbearably hot. Sweat poured down Lance's forehead and burned his eyes. And still the infra-red-ray telescope hung on, guiding Lance and his men down towards the unknown mountains of Tibet.

As the men flew closer and closer to the coordinates, the weather cleared somewhat and a patch of relatively flat ground came into view, perfect for landing.

However, as the planes glided down toward the clearing, the three flying aces heard a steadily growing whine coming from outside their cockpits. Peering up through his canopy, Lance observed something unbelievable.

Above the three planes there floated what seemed to be a dirigible! But it was like no dirigible that Lance had ever seen. Instead of the traditional cigar shape, this floating behemoth was circular, painted a matte black, and didn't seem to have any visible guidance systems.

Great shimmers emanated in waves from the floating airship, and could be seen expanding outward through the air. Each time a wave passed through the Skybolt and Skeeters, it grew another few degrees hotter in Lance's cockpit and yet another system failed.

"It's that thing!" Lance yelled into his radio mike, but Red and Buck didn't reply. The radio was dead.

Lance made up his mind quickly. Unless they took out the dirigible—for want of a better term—their planes might be completely destroyed. They could probably still land safely, but the energy waves would turn their craft into slag, and they'd be trapped in the frozen wasteland with no chance of escape.

No, their only option was to attack!

Lance swung the Skybolt up and around in a tight arc and headed straight for the dirigible. Buck and Red saw him, and pulled their Skeeters up and around behind him. Good men!

Lance's Skybolt continued to home in on the enemy dirigible. He struggled to hold onto the controls and clear his burning eyes of the sweat. Buck and Red circled around to tackle the behemoth from different angles, the twin Diesels of each plane straining.

Lance fired his .50 caliber machine guns point blank and pulled up. The others also scored direct hits, and the hovering black shape made no move to evade their fire. In fact, it continued to hang serenely in place, occasionally emanating the shimmering pulses of energy.

The three planes banked around again, and as they approached, yet another wave of energy blasted from the dirigible. It seemed as

Lance's Skybolt II continued to home in on the enemy dirigible.

if it couldn't get any hotter in the Skybolt's cockpit, and yet it did. Lance's hands were starting to blister and he gritted his teeth against the pain.

Lance fired the machine guns again, and as he passed, he let loose with the .30 caliber swivel gun. Banking almost straight up, he looped around and headed downward. The hovering black menace presented a much larger target from above, and Lance fired his .37 mm cannon through the hollow of the counter-rotating prop shaft.

Red and Buck got the idea, and the three began pummeling the floating craft from above and below.

Lance flew by close enough to see various bullet holes tearing through the craft's skin, and yet it must have been heavily armored somehow. A traditional dirigible would have gone up in flames long before now. Lance would have given his eyeteeth to discover the technology behind the enemy craft.

Still, the mysterious vehicle must be taking some damage. It started to descend in small fits and starts toward the ground, and was lurching to one side.

"We've got it on the run," Lance cried, though he knew Buck and Red could not hear him.

As if in response the black airship stepped up the energy pulses. Lance wouldn't be able to hold onto the controls for another minute. His face was red and the skin not covered by his white helmet was burned from the heat. He pulled around for one last, desperate run at the enemy.

Buck and Red also pulled around, and in unison the three aces blazed toward the dark blimp. They had flown together in enough air battles that they didn't need radios to coordinate their attacks. The men were closer than brothers and flew as if they were reading each others' minds.

They all knew this was their last chance.

Lance, Buck, and Red went in with all guns roaring. Large rips finally began to appear in the hull of the great airship, as machine gun slugs traced lines across it. Holes were blasted in the side, and smoke was pouring out. Again and again, the Skybolt's guns tore at the enemy, while the two Skeeters relentlessly pounded away with their cannon.

At last flames erupted from the craters opened up in the black dirigible's armored skin. Lance and his men tore away from the airship as it finally exploded in an inferno of fire and debris.

However, the enemy wasn't quite done with Lance, Red, and Buck. As the shock waves of the explosion reached the three planes, so did one final, massive energy pulse.

The pulse rocked the three planes as if they were tiny toy sailboats adrift in the ocean. The three pilots struggled with almost useless controls to put their craft into a safe glide and aimed for the clearing between towering mountain tops.

Somehow the Skybolt II and two Skeeters hit the ground safely and slid across the ice field, finally coming to rest in an immense snow drift.

Lance almost blacked out from the pain of his burns, but managed to open the catches on the cockpit canopy, and climbed out. He slid out of the cockpit to the ground and rolled to a stop, the frigid air and snow cooling his burned flesh. He saw Buck and Red doing the same, but was too exhausted to move and check on them.

The metal of the planes contracted rapidly as it cooled, popping and cracking.

Finally Lance stirred. Buck and Red were still lying prone in the snow, and Lance began to make his way over to them.

As he trudged through the snow, however, something sticking out of the large drift caught his eye, and he made his way toward it.

It was a red wing. A wing from a Spad, of all things.

Excitedly, Lance set to clearing the snow away, shortly uncovering a Liberty engine, which appeared to be mounted on a Fokker D-7 fuselage.

"Buck, Red, come here!" Lance shouted.

The other two men roused themselves, and despite their injuries made their way over to Lance and his discovery.

The three set to work clearing more of the plane, and uncovered enough to see that it mounted all types of guns—Spandaus, Vickers, and Lewis.

"It must have been recently uncovered by drifting, blowing snow.

I've never seen anything like it," Lance said.

Red and Buck exchanged glances.

"We have," the two men said reverently, almost in unison.

Lance looked at them sharply, asking, "You mean—?"

However, his query cut short as he saw behind his two fellow pilots. In their concentration to uncover the fantastic plane, they had not been paying attention. Lance, Buck, and Red were surrounded by figures covered head-to-toe in furs and cold-weather gear.

Lance took a step forward. "Who—?"

A greenish gas came wisping out of long sticks that the figures carried. The gas smelled faintly of mimosa.

"You will come with us now," a woman's voice said. Star and his men felt disconnected from their bodies.

"We will come with you now," the ace pilots intoned dully.

The group, including Lance and his men, moved off toward a light which seemed to wink and shimmer within a nearby crevasse.

And that was all that Lance, Buck, and Red remembered.

✚

Lance awoke with a start. Sunlight beat in upon him, warming his face. He quickly pushed himself up from the cot on which he had been sleeping, and then groaned, holding his head in his hands.

"Slowly, slowly. The effects of the gas will wear off shortly," came a calm, deep voice.

Lance looked up. He was in a cell of brick and stone. A large wooden door had a small window set high off the floor. The window had metal bars to prevent anyone from slipping through it.

The wall opposite the door also held a window, larger, and likewise barred. A small sink was mounted on the third wall, opposite Lance's cot. Several other cots were mounted against the cell walls. Buck and Red lay upon them, still quietly snoring.

A fourth man sat upon another cot, and it was he who had spoken. His skin was deeply tanned and his hair was graying. He was dressed in long yellow Asian silks. A pyramid-shaped pendant hung from his neck. He bowed deeply to Lance.

Lance nodded, but his immediate concern was his friends. He rushed over to check on them, a look of concern passing over his bronzed face.

"Your friends are well," the stranger said.

Lance checked and confirmed that Buck and Red seemed to be healthy enough. Their burns looked completely healed. But he knew they must be exhausted and let them sleep.

Lance was tremendously relieved. He had lost too many close friends and compatriots in the past few years.

He looked down at his own hands. They were also completely healed. Not a trace of the blisters and burns remained.

"Yes, you received excellent medical care before you were brought here, or so I am told. Our captors have access to very advanced medical science," the man said.

"Who are you," Lance asked, turning back to the yellow-robed man. "And where are we?"

"My name is Too'an. You are in the city of Kunlun."

"City? I don't understand. We were high in the mountains of Tibet."

"You still are. See for yourself." Too'an gestured toward the window.

Lance got up and peered outside. What he saw took his breath away.

As Too'an had said, it was a city. Magnificent temples and monumental buildings covered in intricate carvings were interspersed with acres and acres of botanical gardens. In the distance, Lance saw farmland at the edge of the city. Beyond that, sharp, snow-capped peaks surrounded the city, which seemed to lie in an expansive valley.

Palm trees lined the streets, along which people of every shape, color, and age walked. Like Too'an, the citizens of Kunlun were dressed in silks of varying lengths and colors, although most seemed to prefer bright reds, blues, and yellows.

The brightly colored garb that Kunlun's residents wore might have implied a happy populace, but Lance saw no evidence of that. In fact, most of the people looked downright grim. He turned back to Too'an.

"This is amazing," Lance said. "A whole city, completely hidden from the rest of the world! But what of the cold, the snow?"

"An irregularity in weather patterns provides a very temperate climate. We receive just the right amount of rain, and very little snow and ill-weather. Kunlun is protected from the rest of the world."

"It looks like a paradise…"

"Yes," Too'an replied, "and it *was* a paradise, until recently."

"I see. I have to admit"—Lance gestured outside—"those people don't look very happy."

"For uncounted years, Kunlun has existed quietly, protected from the influences of the outside world. Her people were safe, happy, and co-existed in peace."

"And then?"

"Every ten years or so, Kunlun becomes visible to the outside world. Or perhaps I should say 'accessible' rather than 'visible.' Even during those rare times when one can reach Kunlun, it's an overstatement to say that it is visible."

"In the mountains, the snow… I remember a faint, winking light in a crevasse between two peaks," Lance said.

"Yes, that is the only outside indicator of the way to Kunlun, during those brief periods that one can reach it at all. It is almost… a portal."

"What happened here that's made everyone so unhappy?"

"About two weeks ago, Kunlun once again became reachable by outsiders. And outsiders did reach us. Their ruler has imposed martial law, and imprisoned the highest officials of Kunlun. This was the perfect society, until they arrived," Too'an replied wistfully.

"And you are one of those high officials?"

"The highest," Too'an said, a slight smile crossing his face. "At least, the highest right now. We have a decentralized and rotating system of government. Everyone serves, at one time or another. I just happened to be in charge when the invaders arrived."

"And now," the erstwhile leader of Kunlun continued, "perhaps you could tell me how you and your friends came to be here?"

Lance filled Too'an in on their adventures to this point, concluding with a question: "Do you know anything about Le Faucon Rouge? Did he ever come to the city?"

Too'an paused before answering. "I have heard stories, but I cannot tell you anything further."

Lance pressed the point. "We found his plane buried in the snow, just outside the city. They only way he could have survived is if he came here."

"I'm sorry, I cannot help you—"

Too'an was interrupted be the sound of a key turning in the lock.

The sturdy door opened to reveal a beautiful, exotic Eurasian woman. She was dressed in a long red Chinese gown which was slit up the thigh, almost to her waist. Two large jade earrings carved in the shape of dragons hung next to her pale, elegant neck under her dark hair.

She pointed at Lance. "You come with us now," she said.

"Where have I heard that before?" Lance cracked wryly, standing his ground.

The woman gave Lance an odd look. Was it admiration, or contempt? Then she stepped aside to reveal two gigantic men of East Indian extraction. They stepped into the cell and took Lance by each arm.

Lance went.

✚

The throne room—for that was essentially what it had been converted into from one of Kunlun's temples—was bedecked in silk tapestries and scattered jade braziers burning incense.

At one end, a man sat upon a raised dais. He was Chinese, and his emerald silks accentuated his green eyes, which seemed to blaze in their sockets. He was tall, lean, and had the brow of Shakespeare, though his face was Satanic in countenance.

The two giants escorted Lance to a chair at the foot of the platform and pushed him roughly down into it.

The green-eyed man nodded at Lance and waved away his giant escorts. He spoke to the Eurasian woman. "Come, my daughter, sit

*The green-eyed man nodded at Lance and waved
away his giant escorts.*

with me."

She did as instructed, sitting at the man's feet, eyes downcast. He turned his attention to Lance.

"I bid you greetings, Mr. Star."

"Likewise, I guess. You are Doctor Natas?"

Natas nodded with satisfaction. "Very good, very good. I appreciate a man with intelligence."

Lance shrugged. "Don't waste time with insincere flattery. Come to the point. You've been dogging our steps ever since we reached San Francisco. We don't have anything you want. Why are you holding us prisoner?"

"Don't be coy, Mr. Star. We both want the same thing. Midnight Sun. Since we both seek it, it is in my best interests to remove you from the field of play."

"Actually, if you know that much, then you know that we have no interest in this 'Midnight Sun.' I'm only looking for someone who has been missing for many years. A hero of the Great War, an ace pilot."

"Did your so-called 'Great War' have any heroes? I hadn't noticed," Natas said contemptuously. "I know whom you seek. Le Faucon Rouge. I grant you that he was a great flyer. And an even better spy."

"What do you mean by that?"

"My dear Mr. Star, don't you understand? To find Le Faucon *is* to find Midnight Sun. He stole it from me, in 1917. I shall explain.

"Over twenty years ago, scientists developed a formula to what might simplistically be called a super-bomb. I had thought the secret of this bomb, the Midnight Sun, to be buried under the sands of Egypt, and was content to leave it so. As long as the Western powers did not have it, I had no need of it.

"However, I soon found that an American agent had also discovered the secret and escaped to Europe with the intent of delivering it to his superiors. Before this man could reveal the secret, he was framed and branded a traitor. I arranged for this. Unable to deliver his information without facing a firing squad, he escaped and flew during the Great War, biding his time for when he was cleared and could deliver his information. Again, I was satisfied to leave this situation alone. Le Faucon could not deliver his information. I did not need it, and if the secret died with him in battle, so much the better.

"Le Faucon never was cleared—I ensured that—and with the War's end, he was left a man without a country. Embittered, he eventually made his way to the Far East and was never heard from again."

"Just how do you know the history of Le Faucon after the end of the Great War?" Lance asked.

"Because, Mr. Star, I hold Le Faucon Rouge prisoner here in Kunlun. I have eyes and ears everywhere. We intercepted the American agent's communication to your Mr. Lee, deciphered it, and came to the indicated coordinates. Imagine our surprise, as we searched for Le Faucon, to discover the portal to the legendary city of Kunlun!

"Le Faucon could have gone nowhere else. He was either here, or long dead. So we entered the city. But time is running short. According to my calculations, the portal to Kunlun closes in less than two days. Le Faucon must be made to reveal his secrets quickly."

"Why do you care?" Lance asked, honestly puzzled. "I thought you said you were content to leave the secret of Midnight Sun hidden and buried."

"Times change, Mr. Star, times change." Doctor Natas' voice began to rise, and his green eyes glittered. "The world is at war, once again. Japan invades my homeland. The Axis invades throughout Europe. War rages in Africa. The time has come to put an end to it. I shall use the Midnight Sun to end these petty conflicts, once and for all. We shall have order, and peace!"

Yes, Star thought to himself, *the peace of a not-so-benevolent dictator. Stop the war in Europe and rule the world himself!*

"You can help, Mr. Star. My usual methods of ... persuasion have been ineffective on Le Faucon. He has learned some incredible mental disciplines in his time here. With more time, I am confident I could convince him... With more time, I could learn much from this hidden city, much that could change the world, perhaps as much as the Midnight Sun. But I digress. As I said, time is short. Help me persuade Le Faucon to give up the formula."

"And just how would I do that, Doctor?"

"You are fellow flyers. He is sure to respect that. You can explain to him how the outside world has changed in the past twenty years. The political landscape has changed. Petty dictators have seized power all over the world. They must be stopped."

"Well, Doctor Natas, I'm surprised to say that I agree with you, to a certain extent. The Nazis, Mussolini, the Japanese… they *do* all need to be stopped."

Natas looked pleased. For the first time during their discussion, the woman reclining at Natas' feet changed expression, as disappointment briefly flickered, and then her face went blank again.

"However," Lance continued, "I cannot agree to your request."

"Why is that?" Doctor Natas asked dangerously.

"Because, Doctor, I don't agree with your proposed methods. And to be perfectly frank, I don't trust you. You're nothing more than a glorified gangster, and if this super-bomb is as powerful as you imply, I can't see helping put it in your hands."

Natas' cat-like eyes widened with rage, and he made a visible effort to compose himself.

Finally, however, he did so, and gestured to the two giant East Indians who had been waiting in the wings. "Escort Mr. Star back to his cell."

Natas turned to his daughter, and pointed a clawed finger at her. "You go with them, my dear. Perhaps you can convince our guest of the error of his ways."

She nodded slightly and went with them.

✛

"These men are Phansigars," the nubile girl explained, gesturing to the two giant Indian men as they walked back though dark corridors toward Lance's cell.

"You may better know them as 'Thuggee,' which means strangler," she continued conversationally. "I believe that one of your men,

Mr. Tellonger, was almost strangled to death in San Francisco, no? Perhaps Father would have done better to send these men"—she indicated the giant Thuggee—"rather than his smaller dacoits. But the dacoits are better suited to scaling buildings and silent entry..." she reflected.

"You seem to have an unhealthy preoccupation with different techniques of murder," Lance commented.

"Me? No, my only wish is to enlighten your path."

"Fine, have it your way. I thought the Thuggee were wiped out in the last century. I heard they tried a comeback a few years ago, but some archaeology professor from an Ivy League school took them out. They can't be that tough if a bookworm like that can take them down," Lance taunted.

"Oh, Mr. Star, it is fortunate these men do not understand your language. If they did, even their allegiance to my father would not prevent them from killing you on the spot." She smiled sweetly, and then continued.

"To answer your question, the Thugs were never completely eliminated. They worship Kâli, the goddess of death, and have made a science out of assassination, which suits my father perfectly."

She stopped walking, and turned to look at Lance meaningfully. The two Thugs also stopped and watched impatiently as she spoke to Lance. "The particular Thugs are from the south of India, where, as I said, they are also called Phansigars."

The Thugs glanced at the girl as they recognized the name of their cult. They looked slightly puzzled. They knew the girl and Lance were discussing them, but nothing more.

Lance was also puzzled by the girl's strange demeanor.

The girl continued: "Interestingly, and even ironically, the word Phansigar has been translated as 'deceiver,' and with that piece of information, I would please ask you to duck, Mr. Star, and hold your breath."

With that, she suddenly pushed Lance down and faced the two Thugs. Greenish mimosa gas came spewing out of each of the two large jade dragon earrings hanging beneath her dark hair. Within moments, both Thuggee were motionless, staring glassy-eyed at nothing in particular.

"You can breathe again, Mr. Star. The gas disperses quickly."

Lance exhaled strongly, then took in a fresh breath of air. "What's going on?" he gasped out.

The girl moved to him and embraced him closely, running her fingers through his blond hair. "Can't you tell?" she breathed in his ear. "This is a rescue."

At that, she pressed her body against his, and kissed him deeply. Despite the gravity of the situation, Lance felt himself responding, but he finally was able to break away.

"This is… extremely pleasant," he stammered, "but I need to get to my friends and figure out a way to stop your father."

"You should abandon all thoughts of releasing your friends at this time. Their cell is guarded by more Thugs, and we should leave this area quickly."

"What are my options, then?"

"Your planes have already been repaired," she replied. At Lance's look of surprise, she continued with a smile. "I do have *some* resources at my own command. My father knows nothing of the work done to your aircraft. He has been too preoccupied with getting what he wants from Le Faucon Rouge and leaving Kunlun before the portal closes."

Lance nodded, and then caught himself up short. A look of doubt crossed his bronzed face. When he stopped to consider it, it was a little frightening how quickly he was placing his trust in Natas' daughter. And it probably had more than a little to do with the long legs, the slinky dress, and the red lips which had showered him with kisses.

"Hold on. Why should I trust you?"

She turned back to him, taking one of his large hands in her small one. She pulled him close once more, locking her wild, lambent eyes with his.

"You are right, you have little reason to trust me. But the cold, hard fact of it is this, Mr. Star—Lance. You don't have any other options. I hate my father, and am willing to help you. That's all there is to say. Now, are you coming?"

Lance looked at her hard, then shrugged. She was right. If she turned on him later, he'd deal with it then. For the moment, at least, he was free.

"Yes," he nodded. "Just one more question."

She gave a tiny frown and stamped her foot. "We don't have time for this, Lance."

"Sure we do. What's your name? I can't just go around saying 'Hey, you.'"

She smiled at him again. "You can call me Madame Inga."

⊹

Lance was at the controls of his newly repaired *Silver Skybolt II*. He was bundled up in cold-weather gear, which had been required for the hike out of Kunlun to his plane.

Inga sat behind him at the backup controls. Both wore white helmets and dark goggles against the sunlight which played blindingly over the snow.

"Your people did an amazing job with the repairs," Lance told her.

"Yes, my father has a wide variety of scientists and engineers at his command. It was a simple thing for me to convince a few of them to repair your plane, without notifying my father."

Lance wondered just how she had convinced them, but let it pass.

The silver colored sesquiplane was headed for the chasm between towering peaks, which lead to Kunlun.

"Lance," she asked, "we've made it this far undetected, but that won't last. Now that we're in the air, Father's perimeter sensor devices are sure to alert him. What is your plan?"

As if in response to her question, a dark, round airship, the twin of the one that Lance, Buck, and Red had finally shot down the day before, hove into view.

Unlike the previous ship, however, this one quickly sped after Lance's plane, giving chase.

Lance poured it on. The Skybolt II's twin Diesels fed 1200 hp to the counter-rotating props, and the silver fighter shot forward. Straight at the monstrous, snow-covered peaks.

The black airship sped after it, and like its predecessor, began emitting pulses of shimmering energy.

The first energy wave hit Lance's plane, and sure enough the controls began to glow and heat up.

"Lance," Inga said to him, "we can't take much of this."

"I know, I know! Hang on!" Lance said, pushing the engines to their limits.

The airship, however, closed the distance and another energy pulse hit the Skybolt. The sleek workhorse fighter continued to speed toward the mountains and narrow gorge.

"Lance… the mountains…" It was the first time Lance had heard Inga's voice exhibit anything other than cool, calm control.

"I see them, sweetheart." The black disc pulled closer, and as the Skybolt approached the crevasse, Lance slowed down, allowing the enemy to close even further. The black behemoth was literally 20 feet away from the Skybolt's tail.

"Lance…."

"Steady… steady…."

Yet another pulse hit, but this time it did more damage to the environment than to Lance's sturdy plane. As they approached the mountains, Lance and Inga saw great sheets of snow and ice begin to crack and slip off of the mountains above them.

As far as Inga was concerned, however, the impending avalanche didn't really matter. The Skybolt's wings were two seconds away from being sheered off as the silver fighter's nose entered the chasm.

At the last possible second, Lance flipped the maneuverable fighter plane ninety degrees and it slipped cleanly into the narrow gap between the peaks. Snow continued to fall from the avalanche, but it was falling from above and the Skybolt was outrunning it.

The enemy airship wasn't as lucky. It hit the two sides of the crevasse one second after the Skybolt slipped into it, and exploded in a massive fireball. The falling snow and ice triggered by the avalanche hit the ball of fire and the debris which otherwise might have hit the fleeing Skybolt was deflected toward the rocky floor of the ravine.

"Woo-hoo!" Lance let out a yell of triumph and relief.

"I do so love you American cowboys," said Inga sarcastically, but the relief was also evident in her voice.

Lance nodded, satisfied, and kept the Skybolt on course toward the winking, shimmering light that marked the portal to Kunlun.

⊹

Lance and Madame Inga arrived in Kunlun minutes later. She was puzzled as to their next course of action, but Lance had a plan. Kevin McDouglas and Maurice, Lance's head mechanic, had recently installed on the Skybolt some new devices that Lance invented. No time like the present to test them out.

Lance flew the Skybolt in a circle around the perimeter of Kunlun to get the lay of the land, and then activated his new device. Antennae slid from the wings, and sound waves began to emanate from them.

Lance then pressed another switch, and two miniature versions of the Skybolt dropped out of concealed compartments on the lower side of each wing. The robot planes sped away, each of them also emanating the weird sound waves.

As Lance circled the *Silver Skybolt II* around Kunlun, he flew closer to the ground and noted that his devices appeared to be working perfectly. All around, people were dropping to the ground.

"They're not dead, are they?" asked Inga.

"Certainly not, just unconscious," said Lance. "I'm not exactly sure how long the effect will last, but at least four or five hours."

After half an hour of this, the mini-robot planes returned to the Skybolt and flew under the wings, mounting themselves in their compartments. Lance circled the temple where he had been taken for his audience with Doctor Natas, and landed neatly in the gardens adjoining it.

Lance and Inga investigated, and found everyone to be unconscious. They quickly began tying up all of Natas' soldiers, guards, and assassins. At the prison, they revived and released Buck, Red,

Too'an, and other inhabitants of Kunlun. These, in turn, rounded up the remainder of Natas' men from all over the city, imprisoning them.

It was all over in three hours.

And nowhere in the great city of Kunlun, did anyone find a trace of the sinister Doctor Natas.

⁜

L ance, Buck, Red, and Inga sat in audience with Lord Too'an.

"What will happen to Natas' men?" Lance asked.

"They have no place here," Kunlun's ruler replied. "Preparations are being made to escort them to the portal under armed guard. They will be given proper clothing and provisions to ensure their survival, but they cannot stay here. The portal will close in twelve hours."

"Then we also must make preparations to go, Lord Too'an."

"Please, just plain 'Too'an.' All citizens of Kunlun give you their gratitude. You have liberated our city, and helped preserve our way of life. You should be most satisfied at a job well done."

"And Lance prevented Natas from acquiring the key to the Midnight Sun!" Buck chimed in. Too'an acknowledged this with a nod.

"Father was a fool," Inga spat. "I doubt Midnight Sun was ever here to begin with."

Too'an turned to Doctor Natas' alluring daughter. "We also owe you our thanks, Madame Inga."

"It was a pleasure to interfere once again in my father's grand designs," she replied, a trifle ambiguously. "Lance darling, this fascinating, but with all due respect to Too'an"—she nodded to Kunlun's ruler—"I also must prepare to leave. If you'll excuse me?"

The men stood as she departed Too'an's chambers. "Don't be long, Lance, don't be long," Inga called as she slipped through the doorway.

"I don't quite trust her," Buck said after she was out of earshot.

"Nor do I," Too'an said. "It is well that she is leaving with you."

"I know how you feel. But whatever her motives, she did help me out of a tough spot. If it wasn't for her..." Lance trailed off.

"Well, you guys are all worried about some dame," Red Davis said. "But everyone seems to have forgotten the real reason we came here—Le Faucon Rouge. We never did find him!"

"That's right!" Buck said.

"I did have a chance to ask Too'an about Le Faucon while you boys were unconscious. Le Faucon has never been seen or heard of here in Kunlun. And yet Doctor Natas said he held Le Faucon prisoner," Lance said.

"Mr. Star..." Too'an interrupted. He looked slightly embarrassed. "I have a confession. When you were placed in my cell, I had no idea if I could trust you. You could have been an agent planted by Doctor Natas. As it turned out, you were innocent, but even so the cell could have been bugged."

"Are you telling us that you have news of Le Faucon?" Red asked excitedly.

"Indeed." Too'an paused. "I am he."

"You mean—"

"What—?"

"Le Faucon Rouge—you?"

Too'an held up a hand for silence. "Gentlemen, gentlemen, please. Give me a chance and I'll explain."

"Of course, Captain Rand," Lance replied.

"I am just Too'an, a citizen on Kunlun, now."

"I can't believe we've been sitting here the whole time with Le Faucon Rouge," Red exclaimed, hero-worship evident in his voice.

"Well, let's let him explain what happened to him and how he came to be here. Remember, we need to leave Kunlun very soon."

"Sure thing, Lance," Buck said.

"As you know," Too'an began, "after the War ended, I was still considered a fugitive. My faithful friend, Akis, and I traveled aimlessly throughout Eastern Europe, India, Burma, and China. I'm sorry to say that each passing year brought us lower and lower. I was embittered by my treatment by my own government, and their refusal to believe in my innocence."

"We know you're innocent!" Red chimed in.

"And I thank you for that. To make a long story short, we were on the run after some trouble in Shanghai, and headed toward Tibet. We had engine trouble, the plane went down, and the next thing we remember is waking up here, in this paradise. That was twenty years ago."

"Then Akis is here as well?" Lance asked.

"Indeed. He is quite well and happy, and has a large family. That's really all there is to it. The people who live here are enlightened. Their mental disciplines are amazing. I learned to give up my bitterness over my past misfortunes and begin a new life. As with all citizens, it eventually came time for me to serve Kunlun in a leadership capacity, and here we are."

"You do know, don't you sir... the American government is prepared to offer you a full pardon on all charges?" Buck asked.

"I understand that from what Lance told me earlier about his search for Le Faucon Rouge—me."

"Will you come home with us, Faucon?" Red asked.

"No. I thank you for the offer. I know you are sincere. But my life is here now."

"Sir, I'm sorry, but I have to ask. What about the secret of the super-bomb?" Lance said.

"I am sorry, but I have come to believe that it is a secret to a power that men should not control," Too'an said.

Lance nodded.

"And, perhaps my mental evolution is still not equal to that of my fellow citizens," Too'an continued with a rueful smile. "I find the offer of pardon suspect. I believe that your government is more interested in the super-bomb formula than in righting a past wrong."

The men sat in silence for a few moments. Then Too'an said: "Come, gentlemen, come! This is a time of happiness. You still have helped to prevent a disaster, one that might have had worldwide repercussions, if Natas had escaped with Midnight Sun."

"You're right, Too'an," Lance said. "We thank you for your hospitality. We do need to go, before the city closes off for another ten years."

"Just one last thing, Lance. What will you tell the Americans?"

"They already know of these coordinates. Mr. Lee is a cagey one. I'm not sure if he knew Kunlun was here or not."

"I understand. However, it is better to be prepared. I will warn the citizens of Kunlun to expect visitors in ten or twenty years. We will not be caught off guard again."

"Well, I for one will avoid mentioning Kunlun," Lance agreed.

"And the Midnight Sun? How will you explain your failure to return with its secrets?"

"That one's easy. Our mission was to find you, not Midnight Sun. I will have to convey my regrets to Mr. Lee that Le Faucon almost certainly perished twenty years ago."

Lance chuckled, as they walked out. "I'm more worried about what do to with Madame Inga."

✝

As it turned out, the redoubtable Madame Inga deserted them on a stopover in Hong Kong. Perhaps Lance would run into her again someday. But such thoughts were dangerous; there was no guarantee they'd be on the same side again.

Star, Tellonger, and Davis were flying over the serene waters of the Pacific, when the Morse code radio transmission came in:

Congratulations on escape from Kunlun. Stop.
Do you have the Midnight Sun formula? Stop.
Signed Lee.

The three adventurers flew homeward, without reply.

THE END

Win Scott Eckert first read Philip José Farmer's *Doc Savage: His Apocalyptic Life* at the age of eight, and was instantly hooked. After graduating with a B.A. in Anthropology, and in preparation for law school, he served as a graduate assistant at the Savage Crime College in upstate New York. Thereafter, he received his Juris Doctorate.

In 1997, he posted *The Wold Newton Universe* <www.pjfarmer.com/woldnewton/Pulp2.htm>, the first site on the Internet devoted to expanding upon Farmer's original premise of the related pulp heroes of the Wold Newton Family.

He has also served as an expert consultant on crossovers involving characters from pulp fiction and Victorian literature for an intellectual property lawsuit concerning a major motion picture. He has participated in panel sessions on Wold-Newton studies, pulp pastiches, and crossovers at the Comics Arts Conference at the San Diego Comic-Con International, the 9th NASFiC Science Fiction/Fantasy Convention, the Windy City Pulp and Paper Convention, and FarmerCon.

Win is the editor of and contributor to *Myths for the Modern Age: Philip José Farmer's Wold Newton Universe,* (MonkeyBrain Books, 2005), a 2007 Locus Awards finalist. He has written pulp tales for a yearly anthology of Wold-Newtonish stories, *Tales of the Shadowmen* volumes 1-4 (Black Coat Press, 2005-2008), mostly centered on the adventures of Doc Ardan, a French version of Doc Savage. His other credits include yarns in *The Avenger Chronicles* and *Captain Midnight: Declassified* (both from Moonstone Books, 2008). He is a regular contributor of Wold Newton essays and stories to *Farmerphile: The Magazine of Philip José Farmer,* and he was honored to contribute the Foreword to the new edition of Philip José Farmer's seminal "fictional biography," *Tarzan Alive: A Definitive Biography of Lord Greystoke* (Bison Books, 2006). Win's latest book is *Crossovers: A Secret Chronology of the World,* coming in 2009 from MonkeyBrain Books. He has also written a pulp-inspired novel, which is currently looking for a good home.

Find Win on the web at www.winscotteckert.com.

HOW A CRAZE FOR CROSSOVERS LED ME TO LANCE STAR

As my biography states, I received a copy of Phil Farmer's *Doc Savage: His Apocalyptic Life* in 1975. That spurred me on a two-decade quest to collect all the Bantam Books Doc Savage paperbacks and read them in the order that Phil placed them in his Doc Savage timeline. I succeeded in collecting all the books in the 1980s, except for one. I finally found the last one in the mid-1990s after getting on the Internet.

Farmer's *Doc Savage* and *Tarzan Alive* had also left me with an undying hunger to read and become and expert on all the other characters he had included in the Wold Newton Family tree—The Shadow, Sherlock Holmes, Fu Manchu, The Spider, Philip Marlowe, Nero Wolfe, Sam Spade, Allan Quatermain, James Bond, Travis McGee, and on and on.

So I had this interest in fictional timelines, and a love of pulp fiction. Hang on, this really is going somewhere.

Next was a love of comics. I loved superhero comics as a kid but by the time I reached my early teens, I wanted something more. Dave Stevens' pulp- and serial-inspired *The Rocketeer* gave me that, and more; as many folks may know, *The Rocketeer* features an unnamed cameo by Doc Savage and his aides. And the second volume of *The Rocketeer* features The Shadow.

Pretty soon I began to look for other crossovers and started to compile them into a shared-continuity timeline of my own, which I called the Crossover Chronology and posted online. A heavily revised and expanded version of this is now due to see print in 2009 under the title *Crossovers: A Secret Chronology of the World.*

One of the prominent entries in *Crossovers* is Ron Fortier's own *Sting of the Green Hornet*:

> *May 1942*
> *STING OF THE GREEN HORNET*
> *The Green Hornet (Britt Reid, the grand-nephew of the Lone Ranger) and Kato cross paths with The Shadow and Captain America (Steve Rogers). Also briefly appearing are reporters Clark Kent and Lois Lane, Colonel Nick Fury, and President Franklin Delano Roosevelt. Walter Gibson, biographer of The Shadow, is also revealed to be an agent of The Shadow. Not seen, but mentioned by a couple of Army privates, is Namor, the Sub-Mariner. He is not mentioned by name, but they refer to rumors of a man with tiny wings on his feet who is single-handedly sinking Nazi subs.*
>
> *A comic mini-series by Ron Fortier and Jeff Butler, NOW Comics, 1992, which takes place after Timely Comics' "Meet Captain America." The costumed mystery-man on the cover of issue number four is not Captain America, but his half-strength counterpart, Private Lee Powell, aka the Yankee Commando, who did not receive the final super-soldier injection before the murder of Dr. Reinstein by Nazi spies.*

Of course, our Esteemed Editor, Ron Fortier, did not actually name The Shadow, Rogers, Kent and Lane, Fury, and Namor. Their identities were hinted at in the text and art. Perhaps I was wrong in leaping to my conclusions about these characters' real identities!

"What the heck does all this have to do with Lance Star?" you ask, and rightfully so. Well, it just so happens that in the 1970s and '80s, Lin Carter wrote five books about Prince Zarkon and his Omega Crew, a series of fun, pulp-inspired novels with lots of crossover references. The characters and the books were a tribute to Doc Savage and his Amazing Five.

In the third Zarkon book, *The Volcano Ogre*, several popular aviation characters from the pulps, comics, radio, and serials were mentioned: Ace Harrigan (the son of 1940s aviator "Hop" Harrigan), Barney Baxter, Tailspin Tommy Tompkins, Bill Barnes, and Smilin'

Jack Martin. One glaring omission from this heroic group of air heroes was Lance Star. It was too bad that I couldn't use the *Volcano Ogre* crossover to incorporate everyone's favorite Sky Ranger into the shared continuity of the Crossover Universe.

Flash forward to early 2006. I had struck up an online dialogue with Ron... Okay, actually I bombarded him with admiration about his Green Hornet crossover references, and his recent pulp novel, *Hounds of Hell*, featuring a crossover battle between the Moon Man and Doctor Satan. Coincidentally, Ron hit me up a short time later to contribute to *Lance Star: Sky Ranger.* Which just goes to show that lavishing praise on someone is indeed an effective method of getting more writing work.

Seriously, writing a new Lance Star adventure was about as far from work as you can get. I had a great time reading some of the original stories (now available through the wonders of the Internet), researching the characters and their history, and writing the story. And of course I took the opportunity to add a couple subtle crossover references in *"Shadows over Kunlun."* I had a great deal of fun tossing those into the mix, and those references also link Lance into the larger Crossover Universe continuity, if you're interested in such things.

Flash forward again to April 2008, and lo and behold I finally meet Ron Fortier himself in person at the Windy City Pulp and Paper Con! I had fortuitously brought a stack of promo postcards for the previous, out-of-print edition of *Lance Star*, and left them with Ron at his table. Apparently they went like hotcakes and thus was born the idea of this revised edition. So, welcome back aboard, and keep 'em flying!

Lance Star

Talons of the Red Condors

by
Bill Spangler

Chapter One

First Strikes

For a long time, McDaniel didn't notice the sound. He was thinking about the pyramids again.

The young American had never been to Egypt and really wasn't interested in going. But he had been in Panama for a few months, working as part of the force that operated and maintained the canal. So, when things were quiet, McDaniel liked to do what he was doing now-- stand on a walkway overlooking the Gatun locks and mentally compare this wonder of the modern world with a wonder of the ancient one.

The Panama Canal was engineering on an amazing scale. Decades of work and tens of thousands of lives had been spent connecting the Atlantic and Pacific oceans. The Gatun installation, on the Atlantic side of the canal, consisted of two locks, constructed side-by-side, in order to handle traffic in both directions. The walls of the locks were six stories high, looming masses that reminded McDaniel of the newsreels he had seen of the ancient Egyptian monuments. However, unlike the pyramids, work on the canal was far from over. After 25 years of service, a project to widen the canal had been announced, to make it large enough to handle the warships America would want to send through, if it entered the war in Europe. Someday, he thought, thousands of years from now, scientists would be studying the canal the same way they were studying-- *what the devil was that?*

That was when he heard the sound, a mechanical growling growing steadily louder. And it was coming from above him. Shielding his eyes with one hand, he looked up into the morning sky. To his

143

surprise, he saw an airplane approaching.

The pilot must really be lost, McDaniel thought. Commercial air travel over the canal was forbidden, except over Fort Amador. His surprise grew though, when he realized there wasn't just one plane. There were three of them. They were all biplanes, equipped with pontoons, and they were descending fast. Too fast.

What are they up to? McDaniel wondered. Are they going to--

Budda-budda-budda-budda.

A machine gun! They were shooting at him!

McDaniel dropped to the ground, then rolled over so he could look up. He saw bullets ricochet off the metal railing, shatter a floodlight. Then he watched the biplanes pass over, flying low enough that he could feel the prop wash.

What the hell is going on? he thought. Who are these guys? There are no emblems on the planes. What could they--oh, God, no!

The machine guns barked again, engulfing McDaniel in a wave of fear. His panic grew as he saw the bullets perforate the single-story building that held the control room for the locks. That held his co-workers and friends.

Cooper. Reyes. Spivak. Montenegro. Pike. Bickford. They were all inside. But where were they now? Lying on the floor, gasping their last, desperate breaths? Hiding in the cellar? Did he dare to try to find out? Could he risk it?

With a sickening abruptness, McDaniel realized he wasn't going to be given time to make a decision. One of the invading planes had broken away from the others. It banked into a curve and headed back at him.

He ran, but he didn't run fast enough.

At the same time, on the Pacific side of the canal, two compact locomotives were pulling the freighter *Emilia B.* into position on the Miraflores locks. Each electrically-powered locomotive ran on a track 1,000 feet long, built on top of one of the lock walls. Ships were not permitted to enter the locks under their own power, so they were tied to the locomotives by thick cables and towed into place. An American crew handled the ship while it was in the lock.

On the bridge of the *Emilia B.* , the freighter's captain stood next to Gray, the American pilot, who was at the helm. Another American was in the cabin, along with two men from the *Emilia's* crew.

"Is this your first time through the canal, Captain Ruiz?" Gray asked.

"Through the canal, yes," he replied.

"Well, everything's ship-shape. All we have to do now is wait for the water to rise."

Ruiz smiled briefly. "I have learned how to wait. It is a valuable gift. " The captain was an impressive-looking figure who spoke English with only a slight accent. He was well-muscled and had a full beard, although his hair was thinning.

The American chuckled. "Yeah, I suppose it is," he said. "At least, if you're a sailor." Before he could continue, a portable telephone that had been set up next to the helm started to ring. As they always did, Gray and his crew brought modern equipment on board to provide a direct link between the bridge and the engine room.

However, when Gray reached for the phone, Ruiz said," Don't pick that up."

"Huh? Why not?"

"Because I said so!" Ruiz said, the tone of his voice suddenly fierce and commanding. As he picked up the telephone receiver and dropped it to the floor, he added, "Besides, I can tell you what it is. It is a call for help from your men in the engine room."

"What? What the hell are you talking about?"

In response, Ruiz drew a pistol from the holster on his belt and fired two shots at Gray's co-worker. The man groaned and dropped to the floor.

Gray shouted "You bastard!" and tried to grab the freighter's captain. Ruiz stepped back though, as his crewmen restrained the American.

The captain said, "I told you that I know how to wait. That is true, but fortunately, I don't have to wait any longer. You and your men have brought us exactly where we want to be. Therefore, we no longer have any need of you."

The bearded man fired again, an action that brought cheers from his associates. He silenced them with a gesture, then said in Spanish,

" It is too early to celebrate, hermanos. Take the bodies below deck and store them with the others. We can leave them on board when we scuttle the ship. Now, though, I want you to form your teams and distribute the weapons. Quickly, now! Surprise is still on our side, but there is no time to waste!"

With practiced precision, the members of the *Emilia B.*'s crew went about their assigned tasks. The captain went on deck as two men brought out a harpoon gun and reinstalled it. The gun would be used to fire specially-made grappling hooks, with lines attached to them. The hooks would catch at the top of the lock wall and they would use the lines to scale it. The Americans would wonder what they were doing, but they wouldn't understand until it was far too late, just as they would be taken by surprise by Jones' attack on the Gatun Locks. Here, within sight of Panama City itself, he would restore his country's honor.

"We will be like the pirates of old, Jefe!" a man said as he passed the captain. The speaker wore a feral grin.

"We will be more than that," the captain replied, raising his fist to the sky. "We will be Red Condors!"

Chapter Two

Captive Canal

The call from Washington D.C. came late in the afternoon. A high-ranking State Department official telephoned Lance Star and asked him to fly to the District of Columbia immediately, for an emergency meeting. President Roosevelt, the caller said, needed the help of Star and his associates on a matter of the highest importance.

With an invitation like that, Lance did the only thing he could. He departed immediately in his Silver Skybolt, leaving Buck Tellonger, his chief of staff, at Star Field to assemble the rest of the team.

Kevin McDouglas, Star's chief engineer, was already at the field. He was making adjustments to the Big Dipper, Star Industries' newest prototype airplane. Pilot Jim Nolan, however, was in Boston, visiting his parents. Meanwhile, Pilot Red Davis was in Philadelphia, leading a seminar in aerial combat techniques. Fortunately, they had flown in their own planes to their respective destinations, and Buck could reach both of them by telephone. Jim and Buck were both back at the Long Island facility before Lance returned.

Buck had arranged for the group to meet in the conference room in the otherwise darkened administration building. These arrangements included setting up a coffeemaker, which allowed Buck to hand his employer a steaming mug as he walked through the door.

However, before Buck could even welcome Lance back, he and the others realized that their leader was not alone. The blond, blue-eyed Star was accompanied by a slightly older man that the chief of staff didn't recognize. The stranger had dark hair, graying at the temples,

147

and wore glasses. He was carrying a long, cardboard cylinder.

"Gentlemen, this is Clifford Atwater from the Office of Naval Intelligence," Lance said. "He came back with me in the Skybolt."

"In that rear cockpit?" Buck said, lifting an eyebrow. "I'm impressed. There aren't many bigwigs who're willing to spend more than a few minutes in a fighter."

"That's our Buck, the soul of tact, " Jim added.

Atwater smiled briefly, then said, "I've had rougher rides. Besides, time is at a premium. " Like Lance, he was dressed in a flying jacket and slacks, but his jacket was loose and baggy. He must've borrowed it from someone, Buck thought.

"Mr. Atwater is here to brief you on the problem we've been asked to handle," Lance said.

" "Problem' is putting it mildly," he said. "This is a crisis unlikely any the country has ever faced. It has to be solved quickly and without the public becoming aware of it. Otherwise, America will suffer a disaster that could affect us for decades. Mr. Tellonger, if you could get me a cup of that coffee, I'll explain the situation."

Atwater took a large sheet of paper out of his cylinder, unrolled it and laid it on the conference table. It was a detailed map of Latin America, showing the Republic of Panama sandwiched between Costa Rica and Columbia. As Red secured the corners of the map with books, Atwater accepted his coffee from Buck. He took a drink, then said:

"Gentlemen, I presume you're all familiar with the Panama Canal. Since its opening in 1914, it has been an important asset to this country, both militarily and commercially. However, roughly 30 hours ago, we lost control of the canal."

"Lost control?" Jim repeated, a puzzled expression on his face.

"Talk sense, man, " Kevin added.

"Yesterday morning, the locks on both sides of the canal were attacked by an enemy force." Atwater continued. " The strikes may have been simultaneous; we're not sure. If they didn't begin at the same time, they started within a few minutes of each other.

"The control station at the Gatun locks, on the Atlantic side of the canal, was disabled by automatic weapons fire which apparently came from low-flying airplanes. The station at the Miraflores locks, on the Pacific side, was taken over by the crew of a freighter called the *Emilia B.* They killed the Americans who came on board to pilot the ship through the lock. Then they left the ship using grappling lines and other...unconventional...means. After they took over the control room they scuttled the *Emilia B.* , so it would block the channel. We don't have a reliable figure, but there could be as many as 50 people dead."

After a moment of silence, Buck said, "My God...and they're in control now?"

Atwater nodded.

"Who are they? What do they want?"

"That we know something about," the man from ONI replied.

"Late yesterday afternoon, somebody--we don't know who--delivered a box at the office of the governor of the Canal Zone. The box contained a written statement from the invaders....and a severed human hand. They've established that the hand belonged to one of the workers at Miraflores. As for the statement..."

Atwater took off his glasses and rubbed his eyes. "They call themselves *Los Condors Rojos*-- the Red Condors. Their leader just calls himself El Jefe--the Boss. The statement described what they had done and gave us an ultimatum. They say they will maintain control of the canal until they receive $100 million-- in gold."

Buck whistled. "Nice piece of change."

"We believe they can follow through on their threat. After the governor received the message from the Condors, he sent a scout plane to check out the situation. The pilot reported that there were amphibious planes floating on the canal at both locks. They shot him down shortly after that. Personally, I think they let him stay alive just long enough to let us know they had fortified both locks, but that's beside the point. After that happened, the governor telephoned the White House and briefed the president of the situation. Then the president ordered the meeting, with all the experts he could find."

Red, whose nickname came from his hair color, sipped his coffee. Then he asked,

"But who are these Red Condors? Are they allied with one of the countries down there?"

"Not as far as we can tell. We think they're a mercenary group, with pilots from all over the world."

"Turns out that the canal zone government had a handful of reports of mercenaries entering the country, over the last decade or so," Lance interjected. "They just never put it together before this."

"Then the Panamanians aren't trying to take the canal back," Buck said.

Atwater replied, "That would be the equivalent of declaring war. They know they wouldn't win a war like that."

"Do they know about the attack? Are they going to help us?"

"We had to tell them. They're going to share intelligence with us. and help deal with the other ships that are waiting to cross, but there isn't much else they can do. Naturally, they're concerned that any fighting at the Miraflores Locks is going to spill over into Panama City itself, but we've assured them that isn't going to happen." Although America controlled the canal and five miles of territory on either side of it, Panama was an independent country.

Kevin said, "Well, that's a grand promise to be makin'. Does it have any basis in reality?"

"That's where we come in," Lance said. "But maybe I should let Mr. Atwater explain."

"Paying the ransom is out of the question," the bespectacled man said. "Even if we did pay it, there's no guarantee that they would relinquish control. So we need to--neutralize--the Condors in a way that will cause the least amount of damage to the canal and keep publicity to an absolute minimum. This may include locating their headquarters. We believe that you gentlemen have the mixture of skills and resources that we need to do this."

"And since we're a private organization, the government can always deny recruiting us," Buck added.

"Frankly, yes. But there is going to be one direction connection with the government. I'm going to be coming with you."

"Sorry, but that's not the way we do things," Jim said.

"It is this time," Atwater responded. "The president wants me in Panama as his eyes and ears on the scene. He's ordered a gunship to take a position on the Atlantic side of the canal. If, for some reason, you are unable to dislodge the Condors, I have to decide whether to begin off-shore bombardment of the canal. The government doesn't want to damage the canal any more than necessary, but if we have to choose between destroying it or leaving it in enemy hands..." He didn't need to finish the statement.

Buck exhaled loudly. " So, Lance," he said. "What's the play?"

"We're going to need to refuel at least once between here and the canal," his employer answered.

"I can arrange that," Atwater said. "Don't worry about it."

"Kevin, is the Big Dipper ready for a field trial?" Lance asked.

"Aye, she's ready."

"How long will it take for you to load it on BT-4?"

"Load it?" the engineer replied, briefly puzzled. "I...I'd want to double check the launching rack before I said for sure. But it shouldn't take more than two hours." The BT-4, sometimes referred to as just the Transport, was an amphibian plane that Lance and his associates sometimes used as a mobile headquarters. A veritable giant among planes, it had a wingspan of 144 feet and a length of over 124 feet. In addition to a galley, a dining room, and berths for sleeping, the craft contained a compact hangar.

The request for loading the Big Dipper caught Kevin by surprise because the hangar had been the home of the Eaglet, the plane that teenager Skip Terrel flew, until his recent death. To his surprise, he was reluctant to fill that space with another craft, although there was no rational reason not to.

"You've got an hour," Lance said. "You and I and Atwater are going to fly down in the Transport with the Dipper. Jim and Red are going to take their Skeeters. I'll fly the Dipper, once we get to Panama. Buck, I'm afraid I'm going to need you here, to mind the store."

"Get going, " Buck said, making a dismissive gesture. "You're wasting time."

Chapter Three

Angel of Death

Someday, Lance Star thought, people will think about the Panama Canal the same way that they think about the pyramids. There will be so many people traveling by air, and so much freight, that the canal will look like a relic from a more primitive time.

Someday, he thought, this won't be a piece of real estate worth fighting or dying over. Someday...but not today.

Lance was at the controls of the Big Dipper as he followed the canal north from Panama City. Because of the shape of the Isthmus of Panama, the canal actually ran north to south, with Colon, the port on the Atlantic side, on the north end, and Panama City in the south. Below him was the blue expanse of Lake Gatun, an artificial body of water constructed as part of the canal.

Lance and his associates had not been in Panama long. Red, Jim and Kevin all decided to take short naps after the flight down, and before they got their orders from Atwater and the Panamanian governor. Lance was tired too, but he still volunteered for a reconnaissance flight over the canal. He wanted to check out the situation for himself, and he wanted to log some flight hours on the Dipper. Although he had worked closely with Kevin in designing the prototype, Jim had been the pilot on the first two test flights.

The Big Dipper was, in some ways, a follow-up to the Buzzbee, one of the first experimental aircraft that Star Industries had produced. It was designed for vertical takeoffs and landings, but it was much close in construction to a traditional airplane than an autogyro like the Bee. In order for the Dipper to take off, the wings were pivoted to a vertical position, so the twin engines could act like autogyro blades. Once it was in the air, though, the wings could be rotated back to horizontal. The cockpit could hold two people and, in what proved to be a prophetic decision, a .30-caliber machine gun was front-mounted on the plane. Although Lance thought the Dipper's capabilities would be useful for this mission, it didn't have the range of the Skeeters. So he thought it would be more efficient to load it aboard the Transport for the trip. Watching the Dipper being loaded reminded him of Skip, his ready laugh and his inexhaustible string of hobbies.

Kevin, who was standing near him at the time, said, "Did you ever think we would see this happen?"

"Yeah, I miss him too, "Lance replied.

Since arriving in Panama, Lance had already tested the landing and takeoff procedures once, placing the Dipper in a clearing in a tangle of jungle. Now, though, all he could see was water. No, that wasn't accurate. Two biplanes, supported by pontoons, were resting on the surface of the lake. Did the Red Condors have sentries out this far?

Who else would have planes here? All civilian traffic was supposed to be grounded.

A heartbeat later, Lance realized that the two planes were not alone. Below and in front of him, another biplane was climbing skyward to intercept him. He identified the craft as a Sopwith Camel, saw that the fuselage was covered with patches. Old, but well cared for, Lance thought. He couldn't afford to underestimate it, particularly if there was a good pilot at the stick. One pilot had already been lost.

As if to verify that observation, the unknown pilot fired at the Dipper. Lance quickly banked and descended, avoiding the deadly rain. For a second, he wished he was flying his Silver Skybolt. This was the first possible time to have to determine what type of combat maneuvers the Big Dipper was capable of. However, this was the only chance he was going to get.

Lance's move brought him to a spot underneath and behind his attacker. He fired at the plane, but his aim was wide. His shots did

the enemy pilot fired at the Dipper...

not produce any damage. He quickly fired another volley, which nibbled at the leading edge of one of the Sopwith's lower wings. The shots alerted the other pilot to Lance's presence and the biplane went into a steep climb.

Lance decided he needed to gain some altitude. But maybe, he realized, he could surprise his opponent as he did it. He moved the Dipper's wings to their vertical position and the craft shot upwards, lifted by the powerful Star diesel engines. Kevin should be here to see this, Lance thought.

After a few seconds, he rotated the wings back to horizontal. If he could reach the jungle, he thought, maybe he could find a place to hide until his adversary got tired and left. As he glanced around, though, the only thing Lance could see was the Red Condor heading directly toward him. He fired again, forcing the American to put his plane into a steep dive.

A wall of blue seemed to be rushing towards the plane. Lance switched the engines back to vertical, though, before using the usual methods to pull out of the dive.

The Dipper was hovering no more than 50 feet above the lake when it stabilized, but it did stabilize.

At least we won't need any more test flights when we get home, Lance thought, as the Dipper, still in autogyro mode, started to rise again. Only a few seconds passed though, barely enough time to admire his opponent's courage, before he had to avoid another blast of automatic weapons fire. This time, the assault came from a new direction--a second Sopwith Camel, barreling through the sky, heading directly for the Big Dipper.

As he pivoted the engines back to horizontal, Lance saw something that sent a chill through his body. The new attacker, which was also equipped for water landings, swerved in fast to the left, before loosing another lethal volley. The Dipper, now back in its traditional configuration, rose above the shots while Lance's mind raced with dark thoughts and fierce emotions.

Jones here!? It's not possible! Of course it's possible, it's Jones. He's tricked us before, what's one more time? I should've guessed he'd be involved in something like this.

With this new information, Lance realized he couldn't be concerned any longer about reaching the Red Condors' installation. His first priority had to be getting back to the base, to alert the others that they would be facing Morgan Jones again. Pushing the Dipper's engines to their limit, he raced over the man-made lake. Every sense was alert as he scanned the sky, mentally preparing for another attack from Jones or his original opponent. After a few seconds, however, Lance realized they were going to let him go.

He didn't know whether to be pleased or worried.

"Part of me always knew we'd see Jones again," Red Davis said. "That man has more lives than a truckload of cats."

Clifford Atwater raised one hand and said, "Wait a minute. I've read the government's files on Jones. He's been accused of some suspicious activities, but no one's been able to prove anything against him. Why do you think he's here and why would he be involved with this?"

After a rapid flight southward, Lance landed at Albrook Field, an American base in the Canal Zone. He immediately arranged a meeting with his squadron and Atwater in a conference room near the airfield.

"Jones is just about the worst thing that could happen to this mission," Lance said.

He had turned a high-backed chair around and was sitting with his legs hanging over the sides. "When you said this El Jefe character had recruited pilots from all over the world, I wondered if Jones was involved. I thought--I hoped--he was dead. I was wrong."

"After the war ended, there were a lot of pilots who wanted to keep being pilots," Jim said. "Some of us were lucky enough to find work with people like Lance. Others weren't so lucky, though. They ended up working for gangsters, or two-bit dictators in Africa and Asia. Some of them, like Claw Larson, built real reputations for themselves. But only one of them became a leader on his own. That was Morgan Jones. They say that Jones was rich before the war, oil and emeralds from South America. But he wanted to be richer."

Lance continued the story: " He put together a small army to work for him. Not just criminals-- pilots and mercenaries too. They called him the Angel of Death because nothing can stop him. I think being with Jones gives his followers the direction and sense of strength they want. It's like a secret army and Jones is the man in charge."

"He tried to kill us once in Peru and once in Hong Kong," Red said. "We don't have any solid proof, but we think he was involved with the destruction of the skyliner *Memphis*."

"That's...very interesting," Atwater said cautiously. "And why do you think that Jones is in Panama?"

"Jones is more than just a strategist," Lance replied. "He was one of the best pilots who flew during the war. The second pilot I fought over Lake Gatun made a very distinctive move during the battle. He swerved in fast to the left, just before firing at me. I've only ever seen one flyer do that: Jones."

"Do you think Jones could be El Jefe?"

"It's hard to say," Lance answered. "From what we've been able to put together, we think Jones prefers to work for others. But he's come up with jobs on his own, too.

All I know for sure is that Jones has an amazing amount of resources he can bring to a situation like this. If he's connected with the Red Condors in any way, they're going to be much harder to defeat than we originally believed."

"Not necessarily," Atwater said. " Any resources that Jones may have are useless, if he can't get them to the battlefield. One of the few things that we know about the Condors right now is that they must be receiving supplies from a main base somewhere. I've been talking with the governor and we've decided that our first priority is to find those supply lines and break them."

"Or find the base itself," Red added.

"We think we need to expand our reconnaissance flights to include the entire country," Atwater continued. "I think Mr. Davis and Mr. Nolan should be part of that."

"Gladly," Jim replied, "but it's a lot of ground to cover. How much time do you think El Jefe is going to give us?"

"Naturally, we can't say for sure, but we can tell you this much: the written statement from the Condors said we telephone them at the Miraflores control room. The governor talked to El Jefe and told them we would consider his proposal, but it would take a lot of time to gather that much gold. He said he understood that, but we shouldn't test his patience."

"Sounds like good advice," Lance observed.

Chapter Four

Summit Meeting

Alejandro Ruiz, known to his followers as El Jefe, frowned as he watched the amphibious biplane set down on the canal near the Miraflores locks. He knew that his plan, his vision, was so large that he couldn't expect to execute it without any problems. Over the decades, he had considered dozens of scenarios, hundreds of possible disruptions. Despite this preparation, though, the mercenary Morgan Jones still managed to catch him by surprise.

Earlier that day, Jones had radioed Ruiz with some bizarre news. He had encountered another airplane sent by the Americans, who were apparently trying to gauge their strength at Gatun. He didn't shoot it down, but he did drive it away. For Ruiz, this was a satisfactory conclusion and should have ended the matter. Jones, however, did not agree. He said there were implications to this battle, matters that had to be discussed face-to-face.

Ruiz didn't like the idea of Jones leaving Gatun and couldn't imagine why it would be necessary. After all, was he not still at Miraflores? Had he not allowed himself only a short nap since they had taken the installation over? Still, he had to assume that a man of Jones' experience would not make such a request lightly. So he placed Escobar in charge at Gatun while--

"Surveying your kingdom?" a casual voice asked in English.

Startled, Ruiz glanced around, only to see that the mercenary had joined him at his vantage point, near one of the electric locomotives used to pull ships into the locks. Had he been that wrapped up in thought? It appeared so.

"My kingdom? Perhaps," he responded. "More importantly, it is a way for my homeland to return to power."

"Don't get ahead of yourself. There are still some bumps in the road. That's what I wanted to talk to you about."

"Go on, " Ruiz prompted.

"The plane I fought today---I've never seen anything like it before. Never. The wings could go from horizontal to vertical and back again. It could fly like a plane, and like an autogyro."

"So the Americans have a new aircraft. That is hardly reason to--"

"You don't understand," Jones interrupted. "If this plane was in production, I'd know about it. This is an experimental craft, a one-of-a-kind model. Something like this could come from only one man: Lance Star."

"The American industrialist?"

"He's more than an industrialist. He's an inventor and one of the best pilots I've ever seen." Jones took a deep breath, then continued." I've gone up against him more than once. He's my equal behind the stick, and that's not something I like to admit."

Clearly not, Ruiz thought. Then he said, "And you believe this Star is here in Panama."

"I know he is. I've checked with our agents in the Canal Zone. He's here, along with two of his best pilots. His top engineer is also here, along with a man named Atwater, who is supposedly the president's personal representative."

"Perhaps this Atwater will be more tractable than the governor has been so far."

"Well, I think he can help us," the mercenary said, "but not in the way that you mean."

"What do you have in mind?"

"I think he can help us neutralize Star and his companions. Here's what I'd like to do...."

After Jones explained his idea, Ruiz said, :"I don't like the of starting another operation. Our forces are stretched too thinly as it is."

"I understand that, but Star has to be taken off the board. If we do it this way, it will create the maximum amount of trouble for the Americans."

"Yes, I can see that. Go ahead then. I will tell Escobar that he will be commanding Gatun until further notice."

Chapter Five

Vanishing Act

After meeting with his squadron and Atwater, Lance decided to try to get some sleep. The commander of Albrook Field had turned some unused officers' quarters over to the visitors and, despite his concerns about Morgan Jones, Lance feel asleep quickly.

Eventually, though, he was awakened by a rapid pounding on his door. Snapping instantly to full alertness, he discovered that Kevin McDouglas was the source of the pounding.

"We've got a problem, Lance. It looks like Jones has kidnapped Atwater."

"What? How?"

"Your guess is as good as mine, but it apparently happened on a road between here and Panama City. The commander just told me about it. He's got a car and driver waiting to take us where it apparently happened."

Before long, Lance and Kevin were sitting in an open car, traveling through the already humid Panamanian morning. Their destination proved to be a roadster, guarded by military policemen. The car was resting on its left side, just off the road.

The MP, who identified himself as Corporal Stevens, explained what happened:

" It looks like the kidnappers fired at the car and forced it off the road. You can see bullet holes on this side. They killed the driver. When we found the car, the body was still here, but we've taken it back to the base already."

Kevin said, "The commander said something about a note?"

"I guess you can call it a note," Stevens replied.

He handed Lance a folded sheet of paper which proved to be a map. The folds highlighted a section of the map. At the top of that section was the handwritten notation STAR = ATWATER. Below that, part of the map was circled. Further down, was the warning SUNSET COME ALONE and a single initial: J.

Star unfolded the map and examined it briefly. Then he sighed and said, "Well, that's clear enough. Jones wants to trade Atwater for me. I've got to go to this spot"-- he pointed to the circled area-- "at sunset tonight or he'll be killed."

"You don't believe this, do you?" Kevin asked.

"It's Jones. Of course I don't believe it. But what choice to de we have?"

"We tell him to take a flying leap. We don't let him distract us from what we're here to do."

Lance shook his head. "And let Atwater die? You know we can't do that."

"Listen to me, son, " Kevin said, touching Lance's arm. " You can't let him get to you. You can't make this personal. You've got to think about the mission."

"I am thinking about the mission. All the missions. I couldn't save Walt's or Jack's or Skip's lives, but maybe I can save this one."

Kevin sighed. "What do you want me to do?"

Several hours later, Kevin was at the controls of the Big Dipper as it landed in a clearing in the rain forest southwest of Panama City. As Lance got out of the passenger's seat, he said, "Circle around and come back in about an hour. With a little luck, Atwater will be here. If he isn't, don't wait around. I'll get in touch with you as soon as I can." He smiled momentarily, then said, "Who knows? Maybe I'll get some info on where the Condors' main base is."

Kevin couldn't bring himself to smile. He said, "Yeah, who knows?" Then he closed the cockpit.

For a for a few seconds, Lance watched Dipper shrink, then vanish, in the darkening sky. Then he started to look at the riot of foliage surrounding him. If the prisoner exchange actually did go as promised, he hoped that Atwater wouldn't have to stay here long. On the flight down, Atwater said he had been in Panama once before, but it didn't look like he had much experience in--

His thoughts were interrupted by a rustling sound to his left. That was followed by an even more unusual sound. A woman's voice said: "You're right on time, Mr. Star."

Chapter Six

Hidden City

A moment later, the voice had a face to go with it. A red-haired woman stepped into the clearing and said, "Before we go any further, though, I need you to open that holster and give me your gun. Slowly." She was holding a pistol in one hand. In the other, she was holding the reins of the horse that stood docilely beside her.

When Lance complied with that order, she continued, "And the knife in your boot."

As he handed over the knife, he said, "So you're a Red Condor."

"Moira Buckley, at your service. Your canteen and flashlight too, please." The Condor was a head shorter than Lance, lithe but shapely. She was wearing loose-fitting pants, boots and a t-shirt that left most of her arms exposed.

While the woman placed the confiscated items in her saddle bag, Lance asked, "Where's Atwater?"

"Same place you're going to be," she responded.

"Can I ask you--"

"No, you can't. Hold out your arms." She tied Lance's wrists with a length of rope, then tied the other end to the pommel of her saddle.

"Don't make this any tougher than it has to be," she warned. "I don't intend to ride any faster than you can walk."

"Thank you," he replied. There was no sarcasm in his tone.

The world grew darker, though not cooler. The Condor guided her prisoner with brusque commands, which he quickly obeyed. Once, he nearly tripped on a root because his attention was diverted by the night sky. *So many stars,* he thought. More than you'd ever see in

*"...open that holster and give me your gun.
Slowly."*

New York City or even Long Island. Looking into the sky had been part of his life for as long as he could remember, and that almost never changed, even when his life was in danger.

After a while, Moira said, "Jones was right about you; you're one of the best pilots I've ever seen."

"When did you see me fly?"

"That first pilot you fought over Lake Gatun yesterday? That was me."

Lance replied, "Oh, really? You're very talented too."

"Go ahead and say it. I know you're thinking it."

"Thinking what?"

"You're very talented...for a girl."

"You're putting words in my mouth," Lance said. "You're a talented pilot. Period." More talented than most, he imagined, in order to be accepted in a gang like the Condors.

Moira made a derisive noise, but she didn't argue. After another while, a dark mass loomed in front of the pair. As they approached, Lance could identify it as a lookout tower. Moira took out her flashlight and pointed it at the top of the tower. She flashed it on and off several times, followed by the occupant of the tower flashing his light in a similar pattern. They exchanged a few words in Spanish, and then Moira tugged at the rope holding Lance's wrists, urging him forward. "Consider yourself privileged," she said, switching her flashlight back on. "Not many people get to see this."

With the flashlight beam illuminating their path, they went around the base of the tower and approached what appeared to be two piles of boulders, separated by a narrow opening. "As soon as we go between the piles," Moira said, "I want you to turn left immediately. Stay as close to the cliff wall as you can. The path isn't particularly narrow, but it is dark."

Lance did as he was told and found himself on a descending path. He could make out the outline of massive stone wall on his left.. Although his eyes had adjusted quickly to the night, he couldn't see much on the right, save that the ground dropped away rapidly.

Where were they?

"This looks like a regular valley now," Moira said as they started down the trail. "But El Jefe says that, once upon a time, this was the crater of a huge volcano. The volcano hasn't erupted for thousands of years, but nobody has ever tried to settle here, so that made it a perfect place for *Los Condors Rojos*. A few minutes later, she said, "Look at this," and let her flashlight shine out into the valley. Lance could make out pieces of several buildings.

"Those buildings look permanent. How long have you been here?"

"Me? Just a few months. But El Jefe started this place decades ago. At least, that's what Jones says."

Lance was not inclined to believe anything Jones said. In this case, though, it looked like there might be some truth to it. He encountered more evidence when they reached the bottom of the trail. On his right, he recognized a set of wooden bleachers, with a large platform in front of them.

"What's that?" he asked. "Looks like an outdoor theater."

"I suppose it is, in a way," his captor replied. "We hold meetings there."

Further along, several large openings had been made at the base of the rock wall, while the patch widened to the size of a one-lane road. On the other side of the road was a mismatched collection of drums and barrels. The scene was illuminated by electrical lights, powered by cables that snaked along the ground.

Lance couldn't see inside the openings, but he recognized the scene from the noises and the smells. He was looking at the Red Condors' airstrip!

Moira stopped and dismounted when she saw a man walking towards them. The newcomer was a smiling Morgan Jones. "Hello, baby!" he shouted. "Welcome back!"

They embraced for a few heartbeats, and kissed. So they're a couple, Lance thought. That explains a few things.

As Moira pulled away, Jones said, "Did you have any problems?"

"Not a one. He came like you said he would."

Jones stepped up to Lance, who was still tied to the horse. He said, "It's good to see you again, Star, particularly under the circumstances." He slapped Lance's face, leaving a bright red splotch. "Things have changed, haven't they?"

"Where's Atwater?"

"Don't worry about me, Star," Atwater said as he walked out of one of the hangars. "You really should be worrying about yourself."

Chapter Seven

Double Cross

Atwater stood beside Jones. He was dressed in a short-sleeve shirt and slacks, rather than in the business suits that Lance had seen him in previously. More importantly, he looked confident and relaxed, nothing like a kidnapping victim.

"What the hell's going on?" Lance asked, although an answer was already forming in his mind.

"I suppose I should thank you for bringing Clifford here down to Panama, Star," Jones said. "You've enabled me to kill two birds with one stone. I've been working with Alejandro Ruiz--you know him as El Jefe--for two or three years now, helping him to obtain pilots and supplies, but I've always felt that he wasn't thinking big enough."

"He's holding the Panama Canal for ransom...and he's not thinking big enough?"

"Ruiz is a native Colombian," Jones said. "He was attending college in America when the Panamanians declared their independence. He thinks that Colombia's honor has been tarnished and the only way to restore it is to take the canal back. He's accomplished a lot. But all he's really doing is standing in the way of history."

"History? Who's history?"

"The Third Reich's," Atwater replied. "The National Socialist party's."

"What are you talking about?" Lance said. Glancing around, he saw the look of open-mouthed astonishment on Moira Buckley's face. This was apparently the first time she had heard Jones talk like this. Another Condor walked by, but he didn't acknowledge them in any way. Either he didn't speak English, Lance thought, or he had learned to mind his own business.

"I was stationed in Europe when the Nazis came to power," Atwater said. "I was...sympathetic...to their beliefs and they understood that I would be a valuable resource for them. We soon came to an agreement.

"Berlin had heard rumors of a paramilitary force being assembled here in Panama. I agreed to investigate, while slowing down any investigations by O.N.I. I learned that Mr. Jones here was involved, and he agreed to negotiate with us."

"Very soon now," Jones continued, "El Jefe will be...forcibly retired. I will be the sole leader of the Red Condors. Once that happens, we will receive our payment from the Nazis and take control of the canal."

"We?" Moira repeated.

"I won't forget you, Sweetheart," Jones replied, "or the people who've been loyal to me for a long time. Most of the Red Condors are going to have to fend for themselves, but we will hire some of them. As for the others...well, things happen when you stand in the way of history.

"I told El Jefe that I was kidnapping Atwater, but, as you can see, he was a willing participant," he said to Lance. "He would've come to us eventually, but now we have you as well. Two birds with one stone."

"You're insane, both of you," Lance said. "This will never work."

"Brave talk, but you're wrong," Atwater said. "You're wrong, and you know it. If nothing else, we can lay mines in the canal, make it impassable for months, maybe more.

If things go well, we can make a foothold for the invasion of North America!"

"When were you going to tell me about this?" Moira demanded.

"We'll talk about that later. Right now, I want you to put Star in the lockup. Then tell Pietro he's on guard duty."

As the red-haired woman untied Lance from the horse, Atwater said, "I still think we should kill him now."

"Not yet. He may still prove useful."

Moira pulled him away, before he could hear any more.

Chapter Eight

Escape

The lockup turned out to be a small, stone building, about 500 yards away from the hangars. This area was illuminated only by a few guttering torches, but Lance could see a few more structures and the edge of an unpaved road that he suspected served as the Red Condors' runway.

"Why do you have a jail?" he asked. "Does El Jefe have disciplinary problems with his troops?"

"Not really. But pilots drink and drunk pilots fight. Sometimes, we have to throw someone in the lockup overnight, in order to break up a fight."

"How long do you think I'll be in your lockup?"

"That's up to Jones," Moira replied. She did not seem pleased by the arrangement. She untied her prisoner and pushed him into the stone structure. He stumbled, then dropped to his hands and knees. That led to the realization that the floor of the cell was covered in straw. The only light now was coming through a small window in the wall facing the door, so it took a few moments for his eyes to adjust to the gloom. When they did, he could make out a chamber pot sitting in one corner. Otherwise, the room seemed to be empty.

He sat down in a different corner, his back against the wall. He couldn't evaluate his situation until someone came for him, or the sun came up, which would allow him to examine the cell more closely. So he did the only constructive thing he could do at that moment.

He slept.

A rattling in the darkness soon woke him, though. The door was open again, and a familiar silhouette was framed by the doorway.

"Wake up, Star!" Moira hissed.

"Moira? What's going on?"

"I told Pietro to take a break. We've got to make our move now!"

"Move?" Lance repeated. "What move?"

"Are you coming or not?"

As his answer, Lance stood up and followed her outside. He didn't know how much time had passed, but it was still dark. Fortunately, there was less activity than before.; the stronghold of the Red Condors seemed all but deserted. As they raced back to the hangars, Lance could see the occasional light glowing in the window of a building.

Once, he heard a few notes of what sounded like someone playing the harmonica. No one was out, though, to question them.

Once inside the hangars, they paused near a twin-engine airplane, larger and newer than anything Lance had seen the Condors fly so far. Moira tapped the fuselage and said, "This is the plane we use to drop supplies to our people at Gatun and Miraflores. El Jefe is at Miraflores now. I can put you in a crate with air holes and drop you there. Once they find you, they'll take you to El Jefe. You can tell him what Jones told us. I can't guarantee that he'll believe you, but he might. Anyway, I figure it's the best chance you've got."

For a few seconds, they stared silently at each other. Finally, Lance asked, "Why are you doing this?"

"Why should you trust me, you mean? Fair question. I'm scared, Lance Star. It's that simple. I met Jones two years ago in Dublin. He was exciting and glamorous and he taught me how to fly. To tell the truth, it was even more exciting when I found out what he really did.

"I talked him into bringing me here and I met Ruiz. He told me about some of the things that you Americans did in order to build the canal and I could sort of see why he had dedicated his life to taking it back. But this business with the Nazis...this has nothing to do with honor or justice. This is about power and fear and I don't want any part of it." She smiled, then added, "Does that make any sense?"

Lance smiled in response. "I can sort of see it. But Jones isn't going to be happy when he finds out you did this. And I'm sure I don't have to tell you what Jones is like when he's unhappy. What're you going to do after I'm gone?"

"I'll survive. I always do."

"You probably do," Lance said, "but I think I can repay you for what you're doing for me. After you drop the supplies, go to Albrook Field turn yourself over to the Americans. Tell them where this base is and tell them what Jones has in mind."

"They'll throw me in *their* lockup."

"Probably, but not for long. Once they realize that your information is good, you should be able to make a deal."

"Assuming they'll believe me."

""They'll believe you. Tell them Red's first name is Eric."

"Who's Red?"

"That doesn't matter now. Just tell them that. Then they'll know you talked to me."

"You're asking quite a lot, Mister Star."

"I know that. But I think you know what's going to happen to you, if you stay here."

Again, they stared at each other in silence. Then Moira said, "We're running out of time. Let's get you on that plane."

When he saw the crate that she had chosen for him, Lance thought that exchanging a dark, cramped cell for a darker, more cramped cell was not the best decision he had ever made. However, as she had pointed out, it was the best chance that he had. At least there were some air holes, and the bottom was covered with straw. Also, once he was inside the crate he could follow much of what was going on through familiar sounds and feelings. The roar of the engines coming to life was followed by the bump and lurch of take off. The box shifted slightly as the plane rose to its cruising altitude and was jostled by a patch of turbulence. Finally, he heard the whoosh of incoming air as the cargo door opened. His crate slid across the floor and suddenly, he was falling.

He heard the sound of the landing, then passed out briefly. When he came to, he realized the top of the crate had been removed and that he was looking at the light of a new day. He was also looking at the puzzled expression of a man staring down at him. The man pointed a rifle at him, then said, in English, "Stand up!"

Lance stood up.

Chapter Nine

A Matter of Honor

The unmarked cargo plane landed at Albrook Field without warning. The base commander ordered troops out to ring the plane even as it was screeching to a halt. They ordered the pilot to surrender, saying he would not be hurt if he gave himself up. There was no response for two long minutes. Then a hatch opened and the Americans were surprised to discover that the pilot was a red-haired woman. She told him that she had an important message to deliver, but she would give the message only to Eric, and he had to come on board to get it. This demand baffled the commander but Red Davis knew what the pilot met. He volunteered to meet with her.

The Red Condor with the rifle was one of three men who had been assigned to pick up the supplies. He tied Lance's hands behind his back and escorted him to a one-story building near the Miraflores locks, while the others stored the supplies elsewhere.

There was a bearded man waiting for them. Alejandro Ruiz, Lance thought. El Jefe. Even though he was clearly exhausted, he still looked imposing.

The armed man tied Lance to an office chair, which he put in the center of the room. He took a position near the door as Ruiz said, in English, "I know all of my men. You are not one of them. Who are you and what do you want?"

"My name is Lance Star, sir, and I--"

"You're Star? I thought Jones was holding you."

"He was, but I escaped."

"How?" Ruiz demanded. He towered over his prisoner.

"That's really not important right now. I want to warn you about Jones."

"What about him?"

"He wants to double cross you....to betray you. He wants to kill you and turn the canal over to the Nazis, the party that took over Germany last year."

"I know who the Nazis are, Mister Star," Ruiz replied, folding his arms. "But why would Morgan Jones be working for them?"

"For the same reason he does anything. For the money."

Ruiz said, "Jones is a man of honor--"

"With all due respect, sir, you don't know him as well as I do. Jones and I...well, let's just say this isn't the first time we've run into each other. Honor doesn't mean anything to him. The only thing that does mean anything to him is winning."

The bearded man considered that for a moment. " I know Jones, I've worked with him," he said at last. "I don't know you. Why should I take your word over his?"

"Because this wasn't an accident," the American replied. "I came here on purpose, to tell you about his plans. Why would I allow myself to be captured again, just to tell you a lie?"

"Perhaps your goal is to drive a wedge between Jones and me. It is not something I would expect from your people, but it's not impossible. Answer this: how did you learn about these purported plans?"

"He...he told me."

Ruiz laughed harshly. "And why would he do that?"

" Because he wanted to do more than win. He wanted to make sure that I knew that he had won."

Shaking his head, Ruiz said, "I don't have time for this--"

"Then make time!" Lance shouted. "You can't afford not to. I know a little more about you now. I know how restoring Colombia's honor is your life's work. You can't afford to let success slip away from you now."

After another moment of reflection, El Jefe asked, "Do you have any proof of your wild claims?"

"No," Lance answered, "but I know where you can get some. Clifford Atwater, the president's representative, is at your main base now. But he's not a prisoner. He's representing the Nazis and Jones is treating him like a guest. If you flew back to his base and confronted him--right now, without warning--you could see for yourself."

Ruiz told the man at the door to take the American pilot away. Before he could, though, Lance said, "I'll go with you! I'll go back with you, and if I'm wrong, you can...you can do whatever you want."

Ruiz studied Lance in silence. "I don't know if you're very brave or unbelievably arrogant,:" he said finally. "But we will soon find out."

Chapter Ten

Deadly Ballet

Moira Buckley told Red everything she knew about the Red Condors; Clifford Atwater's true allegiance and Morgan Jones' plans for the canal. She gave him the coordinates for the Condors' headquarters. Red believed her. He even believed that Lance would go to Miraflores and try to talk to El Jefe face-to-face. That type of heroic insanity sounded just like Lance.

He was surprised, though, when Moira ordered him off the plane without any explanation. Tell the others, the troops surrounding the plane, that they had 90 seconds to get out of the way, she said. Red was surprised, but he did what he was told.

The cargo plane took off, without any further communication from its pilot. None of the soldiers were injured, though. And now, Red thought, they had a chance against the Condors.

Most of the airplanes the invaders had at Miraflores were single-seaters, but there was a Curtiss Jenny that had been modified with a machine gun at each of the two open cockpits. Ruiz chose that craft for his trip. He took the rear cockpit while he ordered Lance to sit in the front. Since the Jenny was equipped with dual controls, the leader left his prisoner's hands tied.

Although he tried intermittently to stretch the rope binding his hands, Lance didn't want to take over the plane. At that point, he sincerely believed there was a good chance that they would arrive at the Condors' stronghold and find Atwater free, as he had promised Ruiz. Even if they didn't, the confrontation between Jones and

180

El Jefe would probably cause enough a disruption to give him an opportunity to escape. He just had to be alert enough to see it, when it happened.

As he considered the possibilities, he noticed movement above and in front of the Jenny. "Eleven o'clock high!" he yelled, trying to be heard over the roar of the wind.

"What?"

"There's a plane coming at us! Eleven o'clock high!" The new craft quickly grew in size and Lance could see a front-mounted machine gun erupt into life. Behind him, Ruiz shouted, "Madre de dios!" He skillfully avoided the barrage, however. That move was followed by a blast at the attacking plane, without any noticeable effect.

With a sinking feeling, Lance realized that the newcomer might be an American craft. Planes from the Canal Zone were supposed to be the only ones in the air right now, and it was likely that an American pilot would assume that the Jenny belonged to the Red Condors. Likely...and correct.

"Give me a knife!" Lance said.

"Out of the question!"

"Give me a knife so I can cut myself loose!"

The high-decibel conversation was interrupted by another pass from their opponent. Another turn by Ruiz kept them in one piece, even as Lance tried to come up with a way to communicate with the other aircraft. If he knew he was facing one of his own men, he could tell Ruiz to rock the Jenny's wings in a specific pattern that would tell the other pilot he was on board. In all likelihood, though, Jim or Red would be flying a Skeeter, which would be instantly recognizable.

He didn't know whether Ruiz had a radio in the rear cockpit, and it probably didn't matter if he did. Even if he could convince his captor to use it, it was unlikely that they could convince the other pilot that they weren't the enemy.

"Give me a knife!" Lance repeated. "If I take over as pilot, I can get us out of here!" El Jefe was a better pilot than Lance had expected, but he trusted only himself to elude the American pilot without killing him.

...he grabbed the controls of his machine gun
and fired at Jones' biplane.

If there was a response, though, he never heard it. The enemy biplane approached the Jenny again, and, this time, Lance saw the familiar swerve to the left before more shots were fired.

That's not one of ours, he thought *It's Jones! Somebody must've warned him we were coming!* He heard a bellow of anger and of pain from the rear cockpit "Ruiz!" he cried, trying to look behind him. The leader of Red Condors was trying to pass a hunting knife over to him. "Take--" was the only word he said, before slumping to one side.

Lance took the knife as he thought, *No more, Jones! No more!* He used the knife to free his hands, then took control of the Jenny. Jones was above them, but he wouldn't have that advantage long. Lance put his craft into an Immelman turn. The Jenny climbed rapidly, tracing a curve in the cloudless sky. The first part of the maneuver put Lance upside-down, but he had full control over the unfamiliar plane. As he reached the top of the curve, he executed half of a roll, which put him the proper orientation with the ground.

The instant after he completed the turn, he grabbed the controls of his machine gun and fired at Jones' biplane. Lance thought he could see tatters of fabric trailing from his adversary's upper wing but he realized he didn't get a solid hit. Jones had dropped to a lower altitude, but he still had control of the plane.

Lance's next run proved to be more effective. His shots hit the rear of his opponent's fuselage, leaving a mark like an open wound. Jones' engine went silent for a few seconds, then sputtered back to life. It was only a matter of time now, Lance thought.

Over the next few minutes, he kept Jones on the defensive, perforating his craft with round after round of automatic weapons fire. The mercenary's engine stalled a second, then a third time, as the biplane sunk lower and lower.

Before long, Lance noticed a coastline beneath them. He thought they were approaching the Pacific Ocean, but they had changed directions so many times during their deadly ballet, he couldn't be certain. In any case, he couldn't think about that question more than a few seconds. He charged Jones again, and, this time, he severed the tail from the biplane. A blossom of smoke and flame started to rise. Jones was probably going to ditch in the water, Lance thought, but he didn't have a chance to witness the impact. He had something new to deal with. Another plane was approaching.

This time, however, he recognized the plane immediately. It was the familiar shape of a Skeeter. Lance rocked the wings of his plane in the pre-arranged pattern, and the pilot of the Skeeter mimicked the pattern in response. The sleek monoplane changed course and Lance followed.

Chapter Eleven

Last Rites

Several hours later, Lance was in the middle of the chaos that had engulfed the Red Condors' headquarters. The destruction of the Condors' fuel dump had produced a fireball that had scattered sparks in all directions. These sparks, in turn, had produced another half-dozen fires in the isolated valley. The flyers who remained seemed to be evenly split between trying to fight the fires and trying to escape. No one challenged Lance as he made his way to the hangar caves.

Red had been flying the Skeeter that had found him, and he led Lance back to Albrook Field. Once they were safe, Red explained that he had gone on a scouting mission to see whether the coordinates Moira had given him would actually lead to the Condors' base. He confirmed that they were accurate and was on his way back, when he discovered the dogfight.

Even while Red was in the air, the military commanders of the Canal Zone were drawing up plans to attack the installation, as the first step toward eliminating the organization. At that point, part of Lance wanted to see whether Jones had survived more than anything else, but his rational side prevailed. Liberating the canal had to come first.

He proposed that the best way to hurt the Condors would be to strike their fuel dump as quickly as possible. He was not directly involved in that part of the mission, though. He took the Big Dipper back to the valley and landed during the battle. His target was the traitorous Clifford Atwater. Without Jones' presence, he suspected that the double agent would quickly be abandoned by the other

Condors.

His suspicions were quickly proven correct. As he drew closer to the hangars, a frantic, disheveled Atwater, now without his glasses, ran out of the caves, shouting, "Star! You've got to help me, Star! You've got to get me out of here!"

"Save your voice," Lance said. "You're going to need it when O.N.I. starts questioning you." He punched the spy in the stomach, then in the jaw. He had to drag Atwater back to the plane, but that seemed like an easy task, compared to everything he had gone through.

Although the Americans would never determine exactly how it had happened, they found out later that the Condors had learned fairly quickly that they were without leaders. Resistance at Ruiz's hidden city was weak and unorganized, while the squad holding the Gatun locks surrendered without a fight. A combined task force of American soldiers and police officers from Panama City raided the Miraflores locks and retook them with only a few injuries. The canal itself would remain closed while divers removed the wreck of the *Emilia B.*, but the officials could claim that sinking was accidental, rather than an act of deliberate sabotage. It would be difficult, maybe impossible, for anyone to disprove that claim.

Lance Star remained in Panama a week after his compatriots went home. He still wanted to see whether the Angel of Death could still bring death to others. Searching the crash site and talking to pilots who had been allied to Jones did not produce any useful information. On the other hand, he did learn that Moira Buckley had managed to leave the country.

Although he wouldn't admit it to anyone, Lance considered that good news.

THE END

Bill Spangler's writing background includes both journalism and comic books (which isn't as bizarre as it sounds, since both fields value conciseness and meeting deadlines), His comic book work includes series based on science fiction TV series such as *Alien Nation*; *Quantum Leap*; *Tom Corbett, Space Cadet* and *Robotech*. In addition, he created the pulp-influenced series *Bloodwing* and *The Argonauts*.

Recently, he's been writing essays for the Smart Pop series published by BenBella Books. His work has appeared in *Getting Lost* ; Star Wars *On Trial* and *Farscape Forever*. He tackled a different sort of flying hero in "The Secret Citadel," a short story featuring the classic serial hero, Commando Cody. "Citadel" appeared in the first issue of *Thrilling Tales,* available from Adamant Entertainment.

Bill and his wife, Joyce, live in Bucks County, Pennsylvania, with two ferrets and a dog.

"*Flyboys*"

by
Bill Spangler

I knew about Lance Star before I really knew about Lance Star.

Oh, I didn't know anything about the series itself , until Ron Fortier invited me to contribute to this book. But I discovered I knew a fair amount about Lance's descendents. I grew up with characters like Tom Swift Jr.; Sky King; Jonny Quest; Mike Mars, and Jeff Tracy and his five sons. Experimental aircraft and high-altitude action play a significant role in their adventures.

(For the record, Mike Mars' real name was Michael Alfred Robert Samson. He starred in a series of novels written by Donald Wollheim that were based on the early stays of manned space program. The Tracy family was featured in the *Thunderbirds* TV series.)

What's more, I realized that, in a sense, I had written similar stories. I had spent several years writing original comic book stories set in the universe of *Robotech*, an animated TV series adapted from three unrelated shows imported from Japan. A pivotal part of these stories are the mecha, the exotic vehicles both sides use. Sure, those vehicles were often gigantic humanoid robots, but not always.

I'm not sure that all anime fans would agree with me on this, but I like to think of mecha as any unusual sort of transportation, not just heavily-armed robots. Using that definition, I think the various one-of-a-kind aircraft that appear in the Lance Star stories can be described as proto-mecha. The type of inventiveness that Lance and his crew showed in the pulps is even reflected in the real world today with Bert Rutan's SpaceShip One, the world's first privately owned and operated spacecraft.

Another thing that strikes me about the Lance Star stories that I've read is that Lance and his Rangers were real world travelers, as can be seen in stories like "Sabres Over Siam." That story was one of the things that prompted me to set my story in Panama.

Of course, I had to learn something about Panama, before I could write about it. This is the first time that I've written something that even remotely fits the description "historical fiction," and I can say now that I definitely see why some writers find doing the research so alluring...and so frustrating. Sometimes, knowing a historical fact made a scene easier to stage. Other times, though, the facts stubbornly refused to support the story I wanted to tell. Writing about a world where your characters couldn't always communicate instantly, or couldn't consult the World Wide Web, proved to be more challenging than I expected.

When there was conflict between history and storytelling, history usually won. Usually, but not always. The Red Condors' secret fortress was inspired by a real region in Panama, the Valle de Anton. I couldn't determine whether the valley was actually inhabited in the 1930s, though, so I used the general description of the area, without committing to the name.

Some of my research led to unexpected results. I registered on one web site in order to get a pamphlet about Panama. I don't think the brochure ever arrived, but I did get a chatty e-mail from someone on the staff of a hotel in Panama City. The staffer said the hotel charged $50 a night for a room--$55, if you wanted air conditioning. There was no way that my wife Joyce and I could take advantage of that offer at that time. However, it made we wonder whether I should be plotting a story set in England. Or Japan.

In any case, it's great to have "Talons Of the Red Condors" back in print, and I hope you enjoyed it. This new edition gives me another chance to thank Ron Fortier for asking me to come out and play (and giving me the time to make some revisions in this story), and Joyce, for her love and support.

Pulp Aviation Heroes
& the Rise of the
Model Aviation Press
by Larry Marshall

"There is no one to whom the romance of aviation makes more of an appeal than it does to the boy between seven and fifteen years of age, and these boys are building model aircraft by the millions"
–**Scientific American**, October 1930

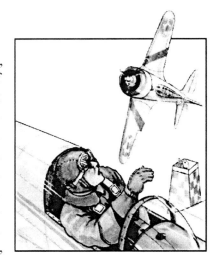

While the '30s were the Golden Age of pulp fiction, it was also the Golden Age of aviation. The rapid pace of aircraft development after WWI caused us to look to the sky for both thrills and entertainment. It was an era where small companies and even individuals were the major aviation innovators, where heroic pilots captured the imagination and a time when everything, it seemed, revolved around aviation.

But it was a young barnstormer named Charles Lindbergh that added a charge to the level of excitement. While it is probably hyperbole to attribute aviation-mania solely to Lindbergh's flight, it resulted in entire industries of gadget-makers' who spilled aviation-related products onto store shelves and into middle-American homes.

Everyone needed an airplane ashtray. Prior to Lindbergh's flight, airplanes in the toy market were nearly non-existent but following it, toy airplanes were everywhere. The "Lindbergh phenomenon" has been a subject of considerable, though puzzled, study by sociologists.

. The flames of passion for things aviation were fanned by the Bendix and Thompson Trophy air races, centered in Cleveland, which were equivalent to today's NASCAR circuit in terms of interest and attendance. The names Steve Whitman, Jim Hazlip, Matty Laird, Jimmy Doolittle and the Granville Brothers were as well known as Earnhardt, Petty and Gordon are today. Brightly colored aircraft, mostly built by small companies and flown by people considered the legends of their day competed and used the latest and greatest technologies in that pursuit.Results of these races were front-page news.

Model aviation was also growing by leaps and bounds in the early30s; fueled by heavily sponsored events by the US military, oil companies and major newspaper publishers. Like the Tom Mix Straight-Shooters Club, used to sell breakfast cereal, other marketing campaigns featured aviation with full knowledge that the way to a parent's pockets was through their children.

These marketing programs were not unlike those of today. Skelly Oil sponsored an "Air Adventures of Jimmy Allen" program and formed the Jimmy Allen Flying Club. Kids would coerce their parents to fill up the local flivver at a Skelly gas station. For their sales efforts the kids were given a "flight lesson" which they would complete. Once they completed five lessons they were rewarded with a rubber-powered model airplane kit with SkelGas written on the tail. At the height of Jimmy Allen popularity, over 600,000 club *Pulp Aviation Heroes* newspapers were being printed weekly and the club's monthly magazine, *Air Battles*, hit a high of one and a quarter million copies.

Not surprisingly, these numbers caught the attention of the publishing world. In 1934, seventeen of William Randolph Hearst's newspapers began a weekly page of "news" for members of a youth-oriented organization the publishers called the Junior Birdmen. Two years later Junior Birdmen membership was well over half a million. Scripps-Howard Publishing, competitors of Hearst Publishing, started the Junior Aviators and gained a membership of 300,000.

Clearly, interest in model aviation, general aviation, and aviation heroes was high and many aviation-oriented pulp fiction magazines hit the streets in the late '20s and early '30s. In 1928, Smith & Smith, one of the heavyweight pulp-fiction producers of the time, launched *Air Trails: Stories of Aviation.* Disappointed with the response, it was canceled in 1930 but as America's fascination with the airplane didn't wane, the title was re-launched in 1932 and was produced for

three more years as a small digest-sized magazine.

In 1934 the magazine was renamed *Bill Barnes: Air Adventurer* and the format changed to that of a full-size magazine. In 1935 the name was changed again to *Bill Barnes, Air Trails* and in 1937 it was renamed to simply *Air Trails.* Possibly more significant was that it was being advertised as "air fact and air fiction" and included both fiction and model plane information.

It was in this book that Frank Tinsley brought *Bill Barnes* to life along with the stunning Bill Barnes aircraft designs—designs that will forever hold a soft spot in the hearts and minds of model aviators, even to this day. Over the '40s and '50s, Air Trails presented more and more model aviation and less and less fiction and became the model aviation magazine that reigned supreme.

During this same time period, a magazine called the *Flying Aces* combined aviation fiction and information about full-size aircraft of the day. Though never as successful as *Air Trails*, *Flying Aces* published a considerable amount of aviation hero fiction, including some Bill Barnes stories. From its pages came an intrepid WWI hero named Phineas Pinkham, who re-fought WWI for many years. Model aviation articles appeared regularly during the later years of *Flying Aces* history and in 1947, *Flying Aces* became *Flying Models*, a model aviation magazine that is still being published monthly. The fiction, however, is gone.

Model aviation articles appeared regularly during the later years Flying Aces history and in 1947, *Flying Aces* became *Flying Models*, a model aviation magazine that is still being published monthly. The fiction, however, is gone.

Model Airplane News is the oldest of the model aviation magazines but also the least significant with respect to pulp fiction history. At its inception in 1929 *Model Airplane News* published some less-than-notable fiction along with its full-size and model articles, but when Charles Grant took over the magazine in 1931, he felt the world was ready for a full-fledged model aviation magazine. He removed the fiction and *MAN*'s slogan became "A course in aviation for fifteen cents a month." It featured articles about both models and full-size aviation. The magazine is published today as a monthly covering radio controlled model aviation exclusively.

While this isn't an attempt to describe the entire history of aviation pulps, no discussion of pulp-aviation magazines should fail to mention the *Tailspin Tommy Air Adventure Magazine*, though there were only two issues ever printed. Tailspin Tommy, however, is well known in modeling circles as an aviator penned by Glen Chaffin and drawn by Hal Forrest. While the magazine failed, the comic strip appeared as a syndicated comic in dozens of newspapers. To my knowledge, Tailspin Tommy is also the only pulp aviation hero ever to make the silver screen as a full-length motion picture.

In 1935 Universal Studios released *Tailspin Tommy in the Great Air Mystery*, with Clark Williams playing Tommy and Noah Berry Jr. as his sidekick, Skeeter.

This history, played out in the hands of young model aviators, has provided a strong link between pulp-fiction of the '30s–'40s and those of us who are the "greybeards" of the model aviation community. Given the passion that model aviators have for model aviation history, I suspect that affection will not die any time soon.

Sky Rangers

Kneeling left to right: Frank Dirscherl, Bobby Nash, Bill Spangler, Win Scott Eckert; *standing left to right*: Rich Woodall, Matt Talbot, Rob Davis, Larry Marshall, Norman Hamilton, Ron Fortier.

Afterword

Ever wonder where the years go and when you aren't looking? Just like that the calendar is saying we're all two years older. It's hard for me to think back to 2006 when *LANCE STAR – SKY RANGER* was about to go to press as the third book from the new, fledgling Airship 27 Prod. At that time Airship 27 Prod. was yours truly and another publisher. Back then we had big plans to revolutionize the pulp community by publishing all new pulp adventures. And we did just that, producing a whopping ten books with the help of some very talented writers and artists along the way.

Now it's 2008 and much has transpired since we launched the old airship. We parted company with our former publisher and recruited a new partner, the ever inspired artistic marvel, Rob Davis. Together Rob and I then partnered with Cornerstone Books Publishers, helmed by Michael Poll. It seemed like Phase Two of our Pulp Revolution was clearly under way. But before we could fully devote all our energies to new and grander projects, we learned that all of our first efforts were about to be dropped by our former publisher. We did a quick strategy huddle and unanimously voted to reprint as many as possible and get them back into print, where they all belong.

Happily that particular process has gone amazingly well and *LANCE STAR-SKY RANGER* now becomes the fourth such reprint. Please note, our intention in doing these new editions was not merely to copy the old files, but to clean them and wherever possible, add new bonus features. The idea is to make the new editions superior to the old ones and with *LANCE STAR-SKY RANGER* we clearly achieved that goal.

This volume contains the four original stories. All of them have been re-worked by their individual writers; some extensively. Our thanks to Bobby Nash, Bill Spangler, Frank Dirscherl and Win Eckert for their efforts. Also to artist Rich Woodall who provided us with his original art files. Nods of gratitude to both Norman Hamilton and Larry Marshall for their fine articles that grace this package.

The biggest change to occur during the past two years is the ownership of *LANCE STAR-SKY RANGER*. In 2007, NeverEnding Concepts, the licensed holder of all the Dutton Press properties, transferred all rights to writer Bobby Nash. Bobby has lots of big plans for our aviation hero. One of these is the first ever, full length *LANCE STAR-SKY RANGER* novel. He has graciously allowed us to publish a sample chapter from that book and we're delighted to bring it to you.

The all new Airship 27 Productions continues to move ahead with dozens of new and exciting pulp books on the horizon. Stop by our internet store and my own website to keep abreast of our plans.

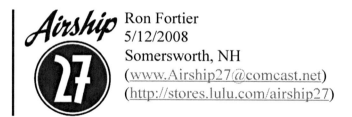

Ron Fortier
5/12/2008
Somersworth, NH
(www.Airship27@comcast.net)
(http://stores.lulu.com/airship27)

The End

PART 3:
October 1941

"Runner"

1.

"This is Ranger One on approach. Requesting permission to land."

"Roger that, Ranger One. You are clear to runway five, bearing zero-mark-two-point-one."

"Ranger One, acknowledged. Beginning approach."

"We'll see you on the ground. Welcome to Miami, Mr. Star."

Lance Star expertly adjusted his course to the airstrip with practiced ease. "Thanks, Control," the pilot said with a practiced smile. "We are five by five and beginning our descent. See you in a few."

Despite his youth, the air ace had earned himself a reputation as not only a top notch pilot, but also as one of the premiere designers of exotic aircraft in the United States, if not in most of the free world. His designs had appeared in magazines and his company's planes were often featured at air shows across the globe.

Even Hollywood had jumped on the Lance Star bandwagon when a major movie production studio recently hired his company to build futuristic looking planes for their upcoming science fiction motion picture. Lance had been reluctant at first, but was swayed into agreement when Red Davis mentioned how much Skip Terrell would have loved working on a movie. Lance signed the contract that same day.

But none of those reasons were what brought the ace pilot to Miami, Florida this day. No, he was there for a far more important reason.

He was there because Betty had asked him to come.

Betty Terrell was a wonderful woman. Not only was she sweet and kind and caring, but she was also resourceful and brilliant. And she was rather easy on the eyes too, a fact that had not escaped Lance's notice from the moment they had first met a couple years earlier.

Betty and her young brother, Skip, had come to Star Field for flying lessons. Young Skip had wanted nothing more out of life that to soar above the clouds. The kid was a natural in the cockpit and Lance's staff immediately took a liking to the youngster. Eventually Lance had offered the youngster a position at Star Field where he did odds and ends while furthering his pilot training.

Having Skip on the payroll had the added bonus of allowing Lance to see Betty again. In an uncharacteristic bout of shyness, the air ace took his own slow, sweet time in asking out Betty. Once he finally found the words, however, she was only too eager to take him up on his offer.

They had been together ever since.

It was Betty's work with the hospital that brought them both to Miami. Betty was in the copilot seat of the LS5 Ranger, a converted fighter plane with a refrigerated storage hold for delivering perishables in place of missiles.

The Ranger was fast, which made it the perfect design for the refrigerated transport. The cockpit was built for two pilots seated side by side as opposed to the traditional one behind the other that was the standard for other planes of similar design.

Since Ranger One was not built for combat, but primarily as a medical transport, Lance and his team has redesigned the cockpit for conversation and to allow the medical personnel access to communications in case they needed to confer with a hospital or medical ship. Having the second seat adjacent to the pilot meant that there was room behind the pilot for one to two passengers. This made the Ranger particularly attractive in times of natural disaster or war. A lone pilot could conceivably return with three - maybe even four if packed in tightly- wounded soldiers or rescued civilians.

"Ranger One on final approach," Lance said into the mic.

"You are clear to land, Ranger One. You may call the ball any time. Your party is waiting for you at hangar five."

"Thanks muchly, Control. I've got the ball. See you on the ground."

He turned to face his copilot, who nervously craned her neck to look out the window at the ground below. "You ready?"

"If I say no, would it matter?" Betty asked.

"Not really," Lance quipped. "Can't stay up here forever. Although there were times I certainly wish I could."

"I know what you mean," Betty said. "I love flying."

"But?"

"But takeoffs and landings..." her voice trailed off. "Those I could live without."

Lance laughed softly. "Don't worry, sweetheart, I'll set us down smooth, just you watch."

Betty smiled. "Smooth talk don't land planes, Mr. Star."

"Lucky for you I'm good at many different things, Ms. Terrell. Besides, word around the water cooler is that I'm something of an expert in these situations."

"Not that you would brag, of course," Betty snorted.

"Not at all," Lance said, tossing his ladylove a wink. "A gentleman never brags."

Lance dropped the landing gear and Betty chewed her lower lip as the plane shuddered slightly as the wheels descended and locked into place. "This part always makes me nervous," she said.

"Sit tight. We'll be down in a second."

The landing was as smooth as he had promised. Lance eased forward on the yolk until the rubber hit the tarmac with a screech. As soon as the wheels touched asphalt, he throttled back and slowed the plane's forward momentum until they were rolling toward their appointed hangar at something more akin to normal speed.

"You can open your eyes now," Lance said without looking at Betty, a knowing smile plastered on his face.

"Ha. Ha." she replied.

Lance motioned toward the small group waiting for them. "That must be Doctor Burnett," he guessed.

"That's him," Betty confirmed. He will take possession of the blood and have it delivered to the hospital."

The plane rolled to a stop and Lance popped the canopy. He unbuckled the safety belt and hopped out of the canopy onto the waiting ladder that the ground crew had rolled into position. The ladder was not necessary to exit the plane as hand and footholds were built into the design. Plus, a side panel opened for inserting wounded on a stretcher if need be.

Lance held out a hand and helped Betty onto the ladder like the gentleman he was. At the bottom of the ladder she was met by the smiling Doctor Burnett, who took Betty's hand gently in his own.

Betty motioned toward Lance as he dropped to the tarmac at her side. "Doctor Burnett, may I introduce Lance Star."

"Mr. Star, this is indeed a pleasure, sir."

"Good to meet you, Doctor. Betty speaks very highly of you and the work you're doing."

"Our Ms. Terrell is most kind," Burnett said modestly as he shook the pilot's hand, the smile still full on his face. "We have been making progress, but there is still much work to be done. Your efforts will greatly aid us in that effort."

"To that end, Doctor, let me show you what we've brought," Lance said as he slipped into tour guide mode. It was the least favorite part of his job, but the pilot was very knowledgeable about the equipment he and his team manufactured and he was a quite adept presenter.

"If you'll follow me," Lance said as he motioned the doctor and his associates to the side of the plane.

Betty began her part of the show and tell as they walked. "The blood that we have brought today came from a series of a blood drives conducted at a series of charity air shows across the country put on by various airfields. Our foundation has raised money and much needed natural resources, such as the blood for use in areas hit hard by natural disasters. After the hurricane that hit this area recently, we felt Miami was the first logical place to deliver. To that end we needed a dependable transportation system to deliver the blood while it was still viable. That's where Star Field came in."

Lance stopped beside the lower side doors of the Ranger and waited until Betty finished. After a nod from her, he pointed toward the locking mechanism. "These seals are used to keep the storage area at a consistent temperature. Temperature changes at different altitudes can cause extreme changes inside the hold, but our new system is designed to counter the effects of differentiating pressures on such delicate cargo. It is a delicate system, but as you will see, the results are well worth the extra care."

"Impressive."

"Thank you, Doctor" Lance said as he popped the first storage compartment open. "We separated the storage area into two compartments as a failsafe in the unlikely event of decompression. While such an event is unlikely, we like to prepare for the worst, just in case."

"Your caution is commendable, Mr. Star," Dr. Burnett said, clearly impressed with the system.

"If decompression were to occur, we would not lose everything. Half a shipment certainly beats no shipment, in the worst case scenario."

"I agree. With your permission, I would like to have my men begin unloading the shipment."

"Certainly," Lance said. "I'll go open the other side."

Lance and Betty supervised the offloading of the blood from the climate controlled Ranger to the coolers used to transport it from the airfield to the hospital's blood bank. Everything went off without a hitch, as they had hoped.

When they were finished, Doctor Burnett approached them, still smiling as he had been when they were first introduced. "I must say, Mr. Star that I am impressed. Everything seems to be in order and we did not lose the first bag. I foresee many medical uses for your incredible airplane."

"We like to think so too, Doctor. We're very proud of the Ranger."

"Would you both join us for dinner tonight? My wife would very much like to meet the famous Lance Star and would never forgive me if I did not issue the invitation."

Lance looked to Betty. His expression told her that the decision was hers. If she wished to stay he would be all too happy to do so.

Betty smiled and nodded.

"We would be delighted, Doctor," Lance agreed. "Let us get the plane locked down and find a place to freshen up and change."

"Very well. I'll send a car around at six p.m. to pick you up, if that's a good time for you."

"Sounds perfect," Betty answered.

While Betty checked them into the airport hotel, Lance rented hangar space and locked the Ranger up tight. He also placed a call to Walt Anderson and informed him of the change of plans, telling him that they would not be back until tomorrow. Walt wished them a good evening and told them to have a good time that everything at Star Field was under control.

Sometimes Lance wondered if things did not actually run smoother when he was not there. A testament to the top-notch team he had assembled, to be sure, but sometimes he wanted to be needed.

The pilot was tired. It had been a busy day. The Ranger had performed far better than expected. With war breaking out on the other side of the world, Lance suspected that a ship like Ranger One would be needed far sooner than anyone anticipated.

And not for the same reasons.

Sooner or later the United States would be drawn into the conflict, he knew. It was not a prospect that the pilot looked forward to, but he knew it was inevitable.

Lance had seen war first hand. He had lost close friends in battle. It was not a situation he wished to revisit.

Thoughts of death and war always brought him back to Skip. Skip Terrell, Betty's baby brother. It had been almost two years since his death, but the memory was as vivid as if it were yesterday. The memory would haunt Lance forever.

But tonight was not a night to dwell on thoughts of fallen comrades and inevitable war.

Tonight was a celebration of life.

And he would enjoy himself.

What the air ace did not know was that he was being watched.

* * *

The two men observed the pilot crossing the tarmac.

As evening approached, the lights mounted on the corners of the hangars came to life, bathing the grounds in a yellowish light so following the pilot's movements was not difficult from the shadows at the edge of their own rented hangar. Star was not trying to hide his destination, which made keeping an eye on him easier. The girl had checked them into a room at the airport hotel and that's exactly where he was headed.

Lance had not noticed the two men, but they had noticed him.

"You know who that is, right?" Marty Taggart asked for the third time.

"Yes. I know who that is," Marty's partner, Jerry Douglas said.

"He was there in Hawaii. That thing with Kiani."

"I'm less worried about who he is than I am about what he's doing here. This can't be a coincidence."

"You sure? I mean, yeah, it was odd that he was in Hawaii when we were there, but how would he know we are here? Do you think Kiani sold us up the river?"

"I don't know, Marty. I doubt it. If Kiani had squealed, it would be Federal Marshals here for us, not some famous stick jockey from New York."

"So what do we do? Should we call off the…"

"No," Jerry said. "Keep an eye on him. If he even looks like he's going to poke his nose into our business again then we'll take appropriate action."

"By appropriate you mean…"

"What I mean is if Lance Star gets in our way again he's a dead man."

To be continued in LANCE STAR: SKY RANGER - 1941: THE ROAD TO WAR, a novel by Bobby Nash. Coming soon.

More Thrilling Reads from Airship 27 and Cornerstone Book Publishers

Find these and other exceptional reading
at your favorite bookstore world wide
and online at: http://www.lulu.com/airship27

COMING SOON IN THE NEXT THRILLING INSTALLMENT OF **CAPTAIN HAZZARD** ...

An evil genius of science has learned how to transform people into throwback savages bent on total destruction and has unleashed them throughout Manhattan.

In the midst of the greatest blizzard ever to hit the gotham. CAPTAIN HAZZARD and his Fighting Five must confront and battle...

The **CAVEMEN** *of* **NEW YORK!!!**

Coming soon from Airship 27 and Cornerstone Book Publishers from Airship 27 and Cornerstone Book Publishers

Coming in Volume Two of:
SECRET AGENT "X"
THE MAN OF A X THOUSAND FACES

4 MORE PULSE-POUNDING TALES OF THE GREATEST PULP SPY OF THEM ALL!

Featuring...
BETTY DALE: GUN-MOLL!
by KEVIN NOEL OLSON

COMING SOON from Airship 27 and Cornerstone Book Publishers

http://www.cornerstonepublishers.com

the Light of Men

A STRANGER IN HELL

It is 1945 and the war is beginning to wind down. Allied Forces are pushing toward Berlin with relentless might and the Third Reich is on the verge of collapse. Still, in dozens of hellish concentration camps scattered throughout Germany, thousands of emaciated men and women are kept ignorant of these events. With over fourteen million already murdered in the gas chambers, the Nazis are all too aware that the remaining survivors could become a serious liability, all of them living proof of their barbaric Holocaust.

Into one of these death camps comes a man named Aaron. Unlike the hopeless, starving men around him, he is strangely aloof and detached from the living nightmare that surrounds them. Obeying orders, falling in line with his fellow prisoners, Aaron methodically begins to learn the camp routines in order to fulfill his own mysterious agenda. Is he an allied spy on some desperate mission? Or worse yet, is he a Nazi collaborator sent to foil any last minute rebellion by the inmates? Having heard rumors that the Allied Forces are getting closer every day, many want to revolt and take control of the camp before their merciless captors can silence them forever.

Andrew Salmon delivers a taut, gripping novel set against the background of one of history's most tragic episodes. He adds a unique science-fiction element that weaves its way through this amazing adventure and drives it to a powerful, heart wrenching climax. The Light of Men is a powerful statement on the human condition and the heroism inherent in all men and women with the courage to endure.

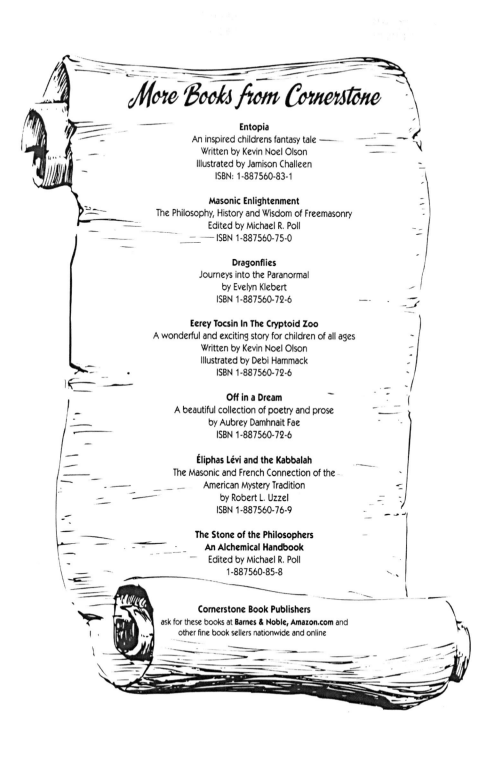

More Books from Cornerstone

Entopia
An inspired childrens fantasy tale
Written by Kevin Noel Olson
Illustrated by Jamison Challeen
ISBN: 1-887560-83-1

Masonic Enlightenment
The Philosophy, History and Wisdom of Freemasonry
Edited by Michael R. Poll
ISBN 1-887560-75-0

Dragonflies
Journeys into the Paranormal
by Evelyn Klebert
ISBN 1-887560-72-6

Eerey Tocsin In The Cryptoid Zoo
A wonderful and exciting story for children of all ages
Written by Kevin Noel Olson
Illustrated by Debi Hammack
ISBN 1-887560-72-6

Off in a Dream
A beautiful collection of poetry and prose
by Aubrey Damhnait Fae
ISBN 1-887560-72-6

Éliphas Lévi and the Kabbalah
The Masonic and French Connection of the
American Mystery Tradition
by Robert L. Uzzel
ISBN 1-887560-76-9

The Stone of the Philosophers
An Alchemical Handbook
Edited by Michael R. Poll
1-887560-85-8

Cornerstone Book Publishers
ask for these books at **Barnes & Noble, Amazon.com** and
other fine book sellers nationwide and online

Printed in the United States
203042BV00002B/781-807/P

9 781934 935019